BOTCHED BRAND

BOTCHED BRAND

TOM WEST

ISBN-13: 978-1-954840-13-3

Published by
Cutting Edge Books
PO Box 8212
Calabasas, CA 91372
www.cuttingedgebooks.com

CHAPTER ONE

Nicked and splintered by a thousand slugs, the piñon stump told a story as grim as the hate-etched features of the cripple slumped in the chair by the cabin door.

Like corrosive acid, that hatred had burnt its mark upon his gaunt cheeks, bitter mouth and pale, sunken eyes. To the few who knew of him he was Crawler Carson, a recluse with two useless, withered legs. What they didn't know was that, decades back, this snarling, helpless hulk threw the fastest gun on the Border. And no one guessed that through a quarter century one obsession—all-consuming—had possessed him—vengeance on the man who threw the bullet that was bedded deep in his spine. Now, at last, he was about to use the weapon that was to give him vengeance.

Crawler made no pleasant picture as he huddled in the shade of the shack, useless legs flopping grotesquely on the ground before him, as though they were stuffed with rags. A week's growth of graying beard bristled his hatchet chin. His restless eyes glittered and his thin fingers clenched and unclenched spasmodically upon the arm of the chair as he leaned forward, eagerly eyeing a blocky young fellow waggling the hammers of two triggerless guns.

Right-left; right-left, the marksman thumbed his colts, whipping lead from the hip with a stuttering roar and deadly accuracy. Finally, a bullet missed the stump and whined off into the brush.

"Git on the mark!" yelped Crawler.

"Hell, Paw, have a heart!" expostulated the stocky young gunman, with restrained impatience. "I'm doggoned gaunted. Ain't I topped fuzzytails and swallowed dust since sunup? Gunsmoke stinks!" He dropped his smoking left gun into a thonged-down holster, morosely plugged empties from the other.

"You'll quit practicin' when you quit missin'——mebbe!" snarled the cripple. "And thet draw ain't smooth enough f'r my fancy. After supper, you work out f'r an hour. Yuh kin pack me in f'r chuck now."

With a grunt of relief, Bill Carson plugged in fresh loads and dropped his remaining gun into leather. He stepped toward the cripple, not ten paces distant.

"Reach!" ripped out Crawler. At the same instant his right hand blurred and a gun jumped magically into his clawlike fingers. It was fast work, too fast to follow with the eye, but he didn't shade the square-set young broncbuster. The younger man's hand moved like a striking rattlesnake and the two hammers clicked back as one. For a moment, each gazed into the black muzzle of the other's gun. Then the cripple dropped his iron back into the holster, without comment.

It was old stuff to Bill. Crawler threw down on him a dozen times a day, regular. There had been a time when he despaired of ever matching the cripple's swift draw—and stemming the current of scorching invective that blistered from Crawler's thin lips. But nowadays he was seldom shaded. When he was, the old-time gunman's curses scorched his eardrums.

He bent, gathered up the cripple with hard-muscled arms, packed him into the log shack and set him on a low chair at the table.

From a lean-to built against the rear wall, a fat Papago squaw waddled in, set smoking venison, baked beans, molasses and steaming coffee on a rough plank table. Placidly, she heaped food on to a tin platter and took it to the cripple. Bill yanked up a barrel chair and went to work on the chuck.

There was little similarity between the two men. Bill Carson was broad in the shoulders, not tall, but tough as a range colt. His lean features were scraped razor-smooth and were unmarred save for a small birthmark, like a bullet scar, beside his nose. He moved quickly, gracefully, on the balls of his feet. His blue eyes were calm and wide-set—and as hard as the steel of his guns. But where Crawler's lips were thin and fretful, the younger man's were firm and tolerant. Short, sandy hair, too crisp for the comb, grew above sober, almost somber features. But telltale quirks at the corners of his mouth hinted at humor beneath the sober mask. Habitually, he wore a look of alert wariness, for which Crawler's eternal gun drill might have been responsible.

Panther Gulch and the peeled log cabin had been home for him as far back as recollection went. His contacts with the outside world were limited to monthly trips south through the hills to San Andreas, almost astride the Border, for supplies. Crawler never failed to go along, too, huddled on the seat of the old buckboard. Visitors to the gulch were nil, for the hate-corroded cripple had long let it be known that anyone who ventured within range of his gun would receive a cordial reception—with a slug. So men avoided the hideaway as they would a nest of rattlesnakes.

The crippled gunman scaled his empty plate across the beaten earth floor and fumbled in a pocket of his stained vest for the makin's. His restless, brooding eyes focussed upon the other's broad back. "I reckon yore ready," he grunted.

"F'r what, Paw?" Bill cleaned the last remnant off his plate, scraped back his chair and slewed easily around. Building a smoke, he eyed Crawler with tolerant indifference.

He was conscious of no affection for the cripple. His mother—so Crawler said—died at his birth. The only mother he knew was Tiata, the squaw, and he had little in common with the plump Papago. Affection was an alien quality in Panther Gulch. Crawler had never given him anything except oaths and tongue-lashings. From the time he could grasp a six-gun in his small fist, the cripple had him blazing at a mark. It was fun—at first, then drudgery, daily drudgery that dragged through months, years. True, he could now hit a target as certainly as he could point a finger, and as fast. But, he often pondered, what was the use? There was no percentage in toting a fast gun. His paw had been a gun shark and look what it got him—a slug in the spine.

Why had he stuck around and taken the punishment of bronc-busting and eternal gun drill? He didn't rightly know. He was close on twenty-five. The world beckoned, but he stuck to Panther Gulch. Maybe it was a deep-seated loyalty to the embittered cripple. Crawler needed him. He just could not ride out and leave his helpless paw. Maybe there was a mite of curiosity in it, too. At times, Crawler dropped vague hints that this unceasing gun drill was for a vital purpose—a purpose one day to be revealed.

This last thought floated through Bill Carson's mind as Tiata moved silently around, collecting dirty dishes, and he met the cripple's frowning stare.

"F'r what!" echoed Crawler. "F'r the job I been readying yuh for these ten-fifteen years. Now lissen! Nigh a quarter century back, son, a lousy buzzard put a slug in my spine and gimme these," he gestured toward his withered legs. "I threw the fastest gun on the Border, warn't an hombre had the sand tuh match cutters with Lightning Lefevre. Time I got out of hospital, the bustard beat it—and I was hamstrung. But I got pards, good pards, son. They been keeping their peepers peeled—year in and year out—knowin' thet Lightning Lefevre never fergets to pays handsome f'r favors. Last trip to San Andreas I got word—the jasper's roddin' a spread near Painted Rock, Arizona."

Bill eyed the older man with growing interest. "Then our name ain't Carson?"

"Nope, knothaid—Lefevre."

"Then why—"

"Aw, quit dribbling, and lissen. When you git a gun rep you git enemies. Right now, they's hombres who'd give their saddles tuh plug Lightning Lefevre. Which is why I got me a new moniker years back and holed up in Panther Gulch."

"How come thet jasper tagged yuh, ef you was so doggoned fast?"

"I got it in the back, didn't I?" snapped Crawler. "Now button up!" He spat out his dead cigarette. "Wal, I swore by every devil in hell I'd even the score afore I died. And I aimed tuh do it through you, Bill. Thet's why I been pushing you f'r years. I wanted you should throw a gun faster'n me, Lightning Lefevre, faster'n anyone you'd come up agenst—jest so you could git Jim Thompson."

The younger man spilled smoke through his nostrils, listening poker-faced to the impassioned, high-pitched voice of the cripple. So this explained the endless gun drill. Crawler was still talking in a sharp, stabbing staccato. And Bill sat silent, pondering upon the poison that had festered in Crawler's mind. Twenty-five years! Paw nursed his hate like an Apache.

Crawler's voice grated. "Yore as strong as a hawse and you got a level haid. I done a good job on you, Bill, there ain't a faster gun either side of the Rio Grande. Now you gotta do yore job—git Jim Thompson, the coyote who crippled yore paw. Bushwhack the son of a bitch, or call him out. I don't give a damn, but *kill him!*" He stopped, panting with virulence of his passion.

Bill sucked his smoke meditatively, steady gaze meeting the cripple's blazing eyes. "I don't take kindly tuh killing, Paw."

"You don't take kindly!" raved Crawler. His voice rose to a hoarse scream. "Ain't you my son? Ain't it a son's job tuh side his paw? Ain't I fed yuh, clothed yuh, drilled yuh f'r nigh on twenty-five years? Ain't I been aching and dreamin' and schemin' f'r this day? And now you got the gall tuh tell me yuh don't take kindly! Tuh bloody hell with yore lily-white feelings! I'm not asking yuh—I'm telling yuh—go git Jim Thompson!" A gun leapt into his bony hand, lined up on the other's broad chest. "Afore Gawd, I'll plug yuh ef yuh show color."

Bill yawned, waved the gun aside with a careless gesture. "I ain't yeller, Paw, and you know it."

"Wal, you gonna git him?" repeated the cripple hoarsely. His face was a twitching mask of hate, his thumb trembled on the hammer.

The other nodded, regarding the embittered Crawler with more curiosity than fear. "Shore!" he returned curtly, rose and stretched, "Want I should pull out f'r Painted Rock right now?"

"Nope!" Exhausted by his passion, the cripple shrunk down into his chair. "Yuh kin drift at sunup. Painted Rock's mebbe three-four days' ride. You gotta cross New Mexico. Git this straight! No palaverin' with the coyote. His tongue's crooked and he'll hogswiggle yuh, shore. Yore moniker's Carson—them on the outside figger Lefevre daid. After yuh beef Thompson, split the breeze. It ain't more'n forty miles tuh the Border—thet's the deadline f'r warrants and posses. Drift back tuh the Gulch easy. And git Thompson in the guts, so as he'll suffer hell afore he checks out."

"Mebbe Thompson u'll git me," suggested Bill, a glint of humor in his cool blue eyes.

"Not ef yuh use the little brains Gawd give yuh—ain't yuh heard of dry-gulchin'?"

Bill nodded.

"Wal, thet's the safe way. Grab a fistful of double eagles outa the trunk and fork the dun. He's a stayer. Thet fancy sorrel of yourn ain't worth a damn on a long drag. Now git tuh work on thet draw!"

CHAPTER TWO

THE COLD THIN LIGHT OF DAWN filtered into the cabin when Bill rolled off the frame of crisscrossed rawhide that served as bed, yanked on his boots, buckled on his guns and stepped outside. He packed a bucket of water from the spring, set it on a bench and splashed the sleep out of his eyes.

Crawler still slept upon a low couch in the corner when he reentered the cabin, gathered up his meager belongings and dropped them into a gunny sack—razor, soap, bandana, shirts, a package of cartridges—set the sack in his soogans and spooled the roll. On the table, Tiata had set another sack, bulging with coffee pot, eating utensils, chow. Throwing the roll on his shoulder and toting the chow, he jingled toward the pole corral.

By the time he had bridled the dun, spread a blanket across its back and cinched on the saddle, a thread of smoke coiled upward from the stovepipe chimney in the lean-to. He tied his roll behind the saddle, hung the grub sack on the horn, and hit for the lean-to.

The squaw set a stack of steaming flapjacks before him as he yanked a box up to a side bench for seat, poured coffee. Smothering the flapjacks with molasses, Bill speculated with inward amusement if all Indians were as sparing with words as Tiata. He never remembered hearing her utter more than a single sentence at any one time.

"I'm drifting, Tiata," he mumbled, mouth full of food.

The squaw nodded, regarded him with dark, fathomless eyes. "You go kill man?"

She didn't miss much, for all her dumbness, thought Bill. "Yep," he grunted.

"You one big jackass!"

"F'r gosh sakes, don't you start tongue-lashing me," he grinned, "I gotta take plenty from paw."

But Tiata had made her speech for the day. Wooden-faced, she moved away and busied herself at the stove.

He cleaned up the flapjacks, rose and hit for the door.

"So long, Tiata!"

The squaw swung around, eyed him unblinkingly, deliberately turned her back upon him.

"What in hell's got into her?" he wondered. Outside the cabin, where Crawler still slept, he hesitated. Should he say so long to paw? Then he shrugged his shoulders and stepped briskly toward the dun. Leaving home, after twenty-five years, was as simple as that—affection just didn't blossom in Panther Gulch, he thought, a trifle drearily.

When the dun reached the brush on the edge of the clearing, he swung around in the saddle for a final glimpse of the cabin. It didn't mean much, but at least it was home.

Tiata stood like a statue in the doorway of the lean-to. He held his right arm high in farewell and saw her plump arm move. Then the brush hid her, as the pony moved through bunched chokeberries. Curious, he mused, looked like she was waving him back. Well, women never had much stomach for gunplay. But Thompson had it coming because of what he had done to paw, and it was his job to feed him a lead pill.

Bill rode all day until wan stars sprinkled the purpling heavens and darkness walled him in. The scarlet glow of a camp fire pricked through the gloom ahead. The plaintive plink-plonk of a banjo floated to Bill's ears and the sound of a deep voice, dolefully singing.

Bill chuckled, raised his head and opened his mouth. A reasonable imitation of a wolf's howl rose into the night air. Abruptly, the singing ceased.

Beneath the willows, Bill glimpsed a lone figure hunkered beside a fire. A banjo lay upon his knees and his head bobbed as he peered into the darkness. At sound of the dun's hooves, he threw an armful of dry brush on to the reddening embers. The dry wood crackled and the flames rose high, bathing the camp with bright, flickering light.

Bill swung stiffly out of leather, beat a thick cloud of dust from his Stetson and glanced around in search of the troubadour. "Go right ahead with the music, mister," he said genially. "It's right pleasing."

A tall slab of a man stepped out of the shadows. Bill guessed he must have stood at least six feet six, and he was as thin as a bean pole. His face was long, bony and expressionless, weathered skin drawn drum-tight over his cheek bones. A sun-bleached mustache curled over the corners of his mouth and humor lurked in the depths of his sunken eyes. He was clothed in faded hickory shirt and stained pants. A red bandana swathed his scrawny neck. A holster dangled below his left hip.

These things Bill noted as the pair appraised each other.

"Good moosic is wasted on some gents," rumbled the tall rider, at length.

Bill remembered his impulsive wolf howl, grinned. "Let it pass, mister. Reckon I got a touch of lobo in my blood. Can I boil up some cawffee on yore fire?"

The stranger hunkered. "Make yoreself at home," he invited. "They call me Fiddlefoot. What might they call you?"

"Bill Carson," threw the visitor over his shoulder, as he bent to loosen the dun's cinches. He glanced back as he lifted off the saddle. The lanky rider's eyes were focused in a stare of frowning intensity upon his nearer gun butt, plain in the firelight. Fiddlefoot caught his questioning glance and hastily averted his eyes.

While Bill watered his pony in a shallow stream nearby, the tall rider struck a few preliminary chords upon his banjo and commenced to sing again.

By the time Bill had picketted his pony, set his coffee pot on the fire and commenced to fry his bacon and beans, he calculated the singer was nearing the fortieth stanza of his song. Fiddlefoot was still going strong when his visitor emptied his platter and stirred molasses into his coffee. "Pour yoreself a cup of dip," invited Bill.

The tall man sighed and carefully laid down his battered banjo. Bill noticed that his right thumb was missing and the hand gashed by an old scar.

"Whar yuh headin' f'r, pard?" he asked.

"Arizona."

Fiddlefoot spat. "Ef the 'Paches don't lift yore topknot, the gamblers u'll grab yore roll. Rattlers, horned toads, sand and skeletons, thet's Arizona—give me hell!"

"So yuh know thet country?" inquired Bill, with interest.

"Pard," growled the tall man, "ain't a corner of this danged country I don't know, from Nevada tuh the Gulf. I been driftin' since I was knee-high to a grasshopper. Reckon I was raised tuh be a tumbleweed, I jest naturally roll along."

"Ever hit Painted Rock?"

Fiddlefoot shot a quick glance at his visitor. "Mebbeso," he admitted guardedly. "You ridin' thetaway?"

"Yep—to punch cows."

"Yeah!" drawled the other, deep-set eyes on Bill's thonged-down guns. "It don't seem a bright notion tuh punch cows at thirty-five and found, when yuh kin draw a hundred and a bonus ef yuh tote a fast gun."

"I don't get yuh!"

The tall rider sipped his coffee, thoughtfully eying the fire. "They's a range war brewin', pard, around Painted Rock. The gun wolves are gatherin' like buzzards. Me, I'm trailin' a certain gun wolf—got a debt tuh pay off." His bony face creased mirthlessly at Bill's blank stare. He held up his thumbless right hand. "A gun slick, name of Lefevre, crippled thet 'gun hand, years back. Some day I'm agoin' tuh meet up with the lobo."

"Lefevre!" Unconsciously, Bill repeated the name aloud. He stiffened at a sudden hunch. "Yuh—ain't—Jim Thompson?"

Fiddlefoot's head jerked up. Across the fire his slitted gaze met Bill's. "Jest what d'yuh know about Jim Thompson?" he grated.

Bill shrugged, eyes wary, "Heard he was hirin' guns—at Painted Rock."

The other's taut features relaxed. "Nope, I ain't acquainted with the gent," he returned slowly, but Bill had a hunch that he lied.

A rattlesnake slithered through the rank grass, its green-black body plain in the firelight. Both men sighted it at the same moment. Two guns leapt out and thundered. But the reptile, beheaded, was a threshing tangle before Fiddlefoot's slug plowed through its coils. "Say, pard," he commented, with new respect, "yore mighty lucky, or almighty fast. And yuh shoot from the hip—Lefevre's style. Reckon yuh never met up with the gent?"

"Nope," said Bill shortly.

"Wal, yuh ain't missed nothin'—Lightning Lefevre's the lousiest, snake-blooded scorpion thet was ever spewed out of the Border.

Bill's lips tightened in quick anger. He checked a swift urge to pull his gun, stared with cold hostility at the bony-faced rider.

"I reckon even a mountain lion has fleas," he returned softly, "but they don't worry him none."

"Cut the deck deeper," grunted Fiddlefoot, with a frowning stare.

"Wal, let's put it thisaways—Lightning can kill his own skunks."

The tall rider stabbed for his gun, but he scowled into the muzzle of Bill's iron before he cleared leather. Slowly, his fingers relaxed and the weapon dropped back into the holster. His brow furrowed in perplexity.

"Why would you side Lightning?" he demanded.

"Mebbe I kind of admire the gent."

"Then it's a shore thing yuh never met up with the hairpin." Humor twinkled again in Fiddlefoot's eyes. "Say, pard, we're loco tuh lock horns over thet coyote. Let it drop!"

"Suits me!" returned Bill indifferently.

Fiddlefoot picked up his banjo, strummed it softly and chanted:

"We're jest two busted punchers
aridin' down the trail,
Two lousy busted punchers
whose gun hands are for sale;
We kin chase the little dogies
and brand the mavericks,
Chouse 'em in the loading chutes
and doctor 'em for ticks;
But we shore ain't nursin' longhorns
f'r thirty-five and found
When we kin draw dinero
f'r throwin' lead around."

He paused and eyed Bill whimsically, "Is thet the way you feel, pard?"

"I reckon so."

"Then what say we string along together?"

"Suits me."

"Shake on it, pard!" Fiddlefoot thrust out a huge, thumbless hand. Bill gripped it, but his free hand lingered close to a gun butt.

CHAPTER THREE

WREATHED BY A HALO of floating, stinging dust, two riders jogged across a flat immensity. Bandanas were yanked up over their mouths and noses and Stetsons tilted low, but still cloying dust particles filtered into their ears, rasped their throats and stung their eyes.

On every side the plain rolled until it was swallowed by the haze of distance.

"Painted Rock!" ejaculated Fiddlefoot, his voice gritty with dust.

Bill squinted across the far-flung flats and saw nothing for a space. Then, through the undulating heat waves, he glimpsed a squat butte, set in the solitudes, far to their front.

He nodded. The stifling heat discouraged speech and his throat felt as though he had been chewing ashes. Hell of a spot to locate a town, he thought.

Steadily, as they crawled closer, the butte grew in size, until it loomed like a great square block, a block built up of countless layers of eroding rock, imposed stratum after stratum—black, yellow, red—slowly crumbling into the dust heaped high at its base.

Fiddlefoot kneed his hock-scarred pony and angled off toward the northern end of the butte. The sun was dropping toward the distant Dragoons and, of a sudden, they rode into shadow. The tall rider pulled rein, lifted a canteen from the horn and gulped greedily, passed the warm water to Bill. "Reckon we earned thet gargle," he grunted. "Drink hearty, we're most inter town."

"Mebbe I'm walleyed, but I can't see no town," commented Bill, eying the precipitous wall of the butte and the deserted flats beyond.

"It lays west of the Rock—they's good water on thet side."

Bill rolled a smoke, enjoying the respite from the burning sun.

"Who you sidin'?" inquired Fiddlefoot.

"I ain't decided—definite."

"Me, I'm for Thompson. They claim the old moseyhorn's tough, but he's a square shooter. Pays top wages f'r guns, too."

"How in heck would you know?" thought Bill, but aloud he said, "Le's look the town over, mebbe Thompson ain't hiring."

They heeled their jaded mounts and rode deeper into the shadow of Painted Rock.

Fiddlefoot threw a quick, questioning glance at the younger man. "Recollect we was talkin' of Lightning Lefevre fust night in camp?" His voice was guarded.

"Yep!"

"I kin put yuh on to a gent who'd pay a thousand—gold—jest tuh locate thet coyote."

"You figger I could earn it?" There was a brittle edge on Bill's voice.

"Nope, pard," Fiddlefoot assured him hastily. "It's jest thet yuh might git tuh learn. Speaking personal, I could use some easy money."

"Wal, I can't earn it."

"Keep it in mind, pard."

Without further word, they circled the eroding pile and Bill at last eyed his goal, the town of Painted Rock. It was no more than a huddle of frame structures, clustered beneath the steep west wall of the varicolored butte from which it took its name. It was, Bill considered, one heck of a town—decayed, desolate, as dead as boothill.

Their ponies' hooves stirred the thick dust of a rutted street, bounded by hitch rails.

"Ef you ask me," commented Bill, "thet range war done dried up and blew away."

"Pard," returned Fiddlefoot, "they's nothing quieter than a sleeping diamondback." He pulled toward the rail outside a dilapidated clapboard saloon. According to the bullet-riddled sign nailed upon its front, it was "The Highway to Hell."

They knotted their reins around the smooth-worn rail, ducked beneath it and pushed through the batwings into a dim, low-ceilinged room. Perhaps half a dozen spurred riders were seated around the tables, drinking bottled beer and whisky.

"Slide over a bottle of snake poison!" boomed Fiddlefoot, bellying up to the bar. "My tapeworms are shore dyin' of thirst."

With wooden features, the bartender set a bottle of bourbon and two glasses before them.

The tall rider poured three fingers, swallowed it at a gulp. Poured again and drank more slowly. Bill trickled a bare two fingers into his own glass, sipped the fiery liquor thoughtfully. Something was wrong, and he couldn't place it. In a flash the answer came—the moment they pushed through the batwings dead silence had descended upon the patrons of The Highway to Hell. He glanced into the back-bar mirror, over the rim of his glass. Half a dozen pairs of calculating eyes were watching them intently. Suddenly, he felt like a mouse surrounded by a ring of slit-eyed cats.

"Riding through, gents?" The barkeep threw the question offhand, as he wiped off the bar, but Bill sensed that every man in the still room was waiting for the answer.

"Nope, I reckon we'll stick around awhiles," rumbled Fiddlefoot.

"The Boxed T's hiring," commented the barkeep impersonally, and Bill could almost feel a prickling sensation as the cold-eyed men behind him waited for the response.

"Ain't thet great!" roared Fiddlefoot. "I'd stake my roll on Jim Thompson."

Like a tight-stretched elastic band that has been suddenly released, the tension relaxed. Glasses tinkled and the mumble of talk again arose. Was it just chance, mused Bill, that Fiddlefoot had picked out the Boxed T hangout to licker in? He glanced through the bleary windows. Across the sun-swept street was another saloon, and they had passed one downstreet. Would it have spelt gunplay if Fiddlefoot had made his declaration in either of those?

The barkeep's face was now wreathed in affability. "Say," said Bill, "pour yoreself a shot and give me the straight of this, we're ridin' on strange range."

"Ain't much tuh spill, gents." The barkeep poured from his own bottle, set on a back shelf. "Jim Thompson located in Grass Valley when there was nothing around 'cept rattlesnakes and 'Paches. He pre-empted the range from Painted Rock to the Black Hills, and most all the water, which was his right. Other cowmen drifted in. They been crowding Jim, laid claim to Boxed T water. Jim don't let go easy, told them to go plumb to hell. Wal, they done got together and announced their plain intention of grabbing if Jim won't give—and Jim sure ain't giving. These gents," he indicated the riders around the card tables with a sweep of his arm, "all done signed up with Jim."

"The fracas started yet?"

"Nope, but the fuse is splutterin' and it's sure close to the powder barrel."

"Whar do we see Thompson?"

"At the Boxed T, ten miles west. These boys u'll ride out before sundown. Best mosey along with 'em. It ain't good business f'r a Boxed T man to ride alone."

"Thet's a right good idea," boomed Fiddlefoot. "Ain't thet so, pard?"

Bill slowly built a smoke. "I ain't in no rush. Mebbe I'll drift out at sunup." He plucked a match from his hat brim, lit his cigarette. "Right now, I crave to give the town a once-over. See yuh later, Fiddlefoot!"

With that he moved toward the street. His tall companion straightened as if to follow, changed his mind and draped his long body across the bar again.

The square shadows of the frame buildings across the street crept toward Bill as he drifted along the plankwalk. He wanted to get away by himself and figure out his next move. Looked like Thompson had a bunch of gun slicks on his pay roll. If he didn't play his cards right there was a big chance they'd get him before he plugged Thompson, and it was a sure thing they would after. He wasn't ready for boothill yet. His problem was not only to kill Thompson but also to make a getaway. His pony was gaunted after four days' grind over mountain passes, through sand, sage and cactus. He needed a fresh horse between his legs if he was to beat pursuit to the Border. Better rest the pony overnight and drift out to the Boxed T at daybreak.

Sauntering downstreet, past water barrels spaced like sentries along the plankwalk, he became conscious of tension around him as tight as that in The Highway to Hell. Few men were visible, and no women. As he passed store fronts he was conscious of scrutinizing eyes through flyspecked windows. A passing townsman threw a quick, questioning glance, and his gaze hastily slanted away before Bill's cool stare.

The rider approached another saloon, The Last Chance, in front of which ponies were tied thick. No hilarity cascaded from its batwings, although men were lined elbow to elbow along the bar. A deep, sullen rumble of voices reached his ears. He glanced at the brands on the tied ponies—Circle S, Rocking T, Frying Pan, P/H. Not one Boxed T among them. It was plain the opposition patronized The Last Chance.

He reached the end of the plankwalk, swung around and turned back, questing for a livery barn in which to stable the dun for the night, and maybe a heap of straw upon which he could stretch out. Three vaqueros banged out of The Last Chance, fifty paces ahead. They were dark-featured, hawk-nosed men, glittering with huge plated spurs, brass-buttoned velvet coats and metal-studded gunbelts. Holstered six guns swung from their sash girded hips. Conchas tinkling around the brims of their wide black sombreros, they jingled in the direction of the solitary gray-shirted rider, like three turkey buzzards strutting toward a drab sage hen.

The resplendent Mexicans occupied the full width of the plankwalk. Bill stubbornly held to the center. Derisively, they attempted to shoulder him aside. But the blocky rider was braced for trouble. Hunched, he thrust between them, spilling one against the hitch rail. Another tripped over his spurs. For a moment there was confusion and flaming Spanish oaths. Bill wheeled to face them—he never could forget the bullet in Crawler's spine. Three pairs of angry eyes smouldered beneath flapping sombreros as they whirled around.

"Theese stranger is a Boxed T cockerel," snarled one, "Mebbe we clip hees wings."

"You and who else?" Slightly crouched, Bill poised for action, half-closed hands brushing the butts of his twin guns.

Scarcely had the taunting challenge left his lips, when two of the vaqueros dabbed for their guns, the third was crowded against the rail.

Right—left, Bill's .44 leapt up and out, roared and bucked with reverberating thunder, before the vaqueros' weapons cleared their holsters. It was like shooting setting hens, thought the rider, with faint contempt. One swarthy Mexican spun around and collapsed like an empty sack, fast-spreading blood-stains upon his right shoulder. The second dropped his gun and grabbed a broken right arm with an agonized howl. The third, eyes distended, stretched his arms high.

Men poured from The Last Chance and streamed toward the group. Further upstreet, Bill saw the Boxed T gunnies emerge from The Highway to Hell and advance in a solid bunch. Startled heads protruded from doorways and windows, but the street was swept clean of townsmen.

Bill backed against a store front, a gun in each fist, while the unwounded vaquero continued to stand as if petrified, arms uplifted. In a few seconds, bleak-eyed, murmuring men circled him like ringing wolves, held at arm's length only by the menace of his smoking guns. The Boxed T contingent was close now, headed by Fiddlefoot's tall form. Bunching solidly, they elbowed through to the encircled Bill, ranged themselves shoulder to shoulder on either side. There was sudden quiet, broken only by the deep moaning of the vaquero writhing on the plankwalk. The powder barrel, thought Bill, his pulse pounding, was due to explode pronto.

A loose-jointed fellow pushed through the thronging punchers, tight-packed on the narrow plankwalk. His features were lean and leathery, and the setting sun gleamed upon his red hair. A town marshal's star was pinned to his loose-hanging vest and he gripped a double-barreled, sawed-off shotgun with two capable hands.

"Hold yore hosses, gents! I'll shore blast the first jasper who jerks his iron tuh kingdom come." He spoke in an easy, amiable drawl.

His quick glance ran over the wounded vaquero on the plankwalk, jumped to the second, sagging against the hitch rail, nursing his broken gun arm, took in the third hesitantly lowering his arms. Then he surveyed Bill's tensed form and the tight-lipped Boxed T men lined up on either side.

"What's the trouble?" His voice smiled, but his gray eyes probed the blocky rider like twin knife points.

"These gents throwed down on me, but I got there first."

A muttering growl arose from the stormy-eyed punchers facing the Boxed T contingent.

The marshal pivoted, swinging his shotgun in a half circle. "Beat it, yuh hairpins," he snapped, "and keep yore feuding outa Painted Rock. Skeedaddle, my trigger finger's mighty itchy."

Still swinging the shotgun, he advanced and men backed uneasily before the threat in his eyes and the death-dealing weapon in his hands. He sure had splenty spunk, thought Bill.

Slowly, reluctantly, the crowd broke and drifted away. The uninjured vaquero steered his two wounded companions downstreet. Fiddlefoot, towering on Bill's right, chuckled. " 'Pears like you blooded 'em, pard!"

The marshal turned back from herding the grumbling punchers and eyed Bill with a cold smile. "How long yuh been in town?" he asked dryly.

"Two hours, mebbe."

"Don't take yuh long tuh start trouble."

"I didn't start trouble."

"Jim Thompson hire yuh?"

"Nope, not yet."

"Wal, he sure won't make no mistake ef he does." The marshal's voice hardened, "Keep them hoglaigs holstered, or keep outta town." With that he cradled the shotgun in the crook of his arm and moved away.

Bill holstered his guns and looked up at Fiddlefoot. "Thet jasper's sure got plenty sand, I was all set f'r a harp."

"Yuh warn't the only one," rumbled the tall man.

"Red Goodmer would tackle a dozen wildcats with his arms tied," threw in a hard-faced gunnie. "He rode for Thompson, way back."

"Le's go!" said Fiddlefoot.

"I'm stickin' around till sunup," said Bill.

"Gawdawmighty, I'd think you'd have had enough gunplay."

CHAPTER FOUR

NIGHT THREW HER VELVET VEIL across Grass Valley.

Bill Carson's boot heels echoed hollow on the sun-shrunken plankwalk. He had located the horse barn. Watered, grained and rubbed down the trail-worn dun, and dropped the liveryman a dollar for a shakedown overnight in an empty box stall.

Right now he was hungry, and the straw-chewing horse tender had spoken highly of Miss Goodmer's Home Cooked Meals. So, ears and eyes alert for possible trouble, the rider sought Miss Goodmer's. The Boxed T bunch had long since hit for the home spread and riders for most all the valley ranches had pulled out of town.

He jingled past The Highway to Hell. Finally sighted a sign, "Home Cooked Meals," tacked over the doorway of a narrow-fronted restaurant that was wedged, like a thin slice of beef between two halves of a loaf, between the barber's shop and a saddler's. Through the hanging fly curtain's he glimpsed a row of round stools spaced down a narrow counter. A kerosene lamp swung from a white-washed beam overhead and a flytrap, shaped like a miniature balloon, was black with buzzing flies. The place looked neat and clean. Brushing aside the curtains, Bill stepped inside.

He hung his hat on a peg, slid on to a stool and rapped the counter with his knuckles. A girl stepped through a doorway in the rear, wiping her hands upon a towel. She was small, shapely and obviously annoyed. Her coppery hair, glinting in the lamplight, was wound in thick strands around her head. She was faintly freckled, with a humorous mouth and pert, upturned nose. There was a devil-may-care gleam in her gray eyes that reminded Bill of the nonchalant marshal. But he read weariness in the sag of her slim shoulders and in the faint lines around her mouth. Her white apron was spotless.

"You're late, rider—I'm closed," she called. Her voice, thought Bill, matched her appearance, forthright and subtly challenging.

"Feller told me you dished up the best chow in town."

"Try breakfast!" she advised shortly.

Bili sighed dismally, "Ain't had a mite under my belt since yesterday sunup."

She moved toward him. "All I have is pie and coffee."

"Yuh bake the pie?"

"Of course!"

"Gimme cawfee!"

She met his grin with a chilled stare, swung around and disappeared into the kitchen. Emerged carrying a large mug of steaming coffee and a slab of dried apple pie. "You'll eat pie and like it," she announced, slamming it down before him. "I should throw it at you, but you'd probably shoot me, being a snake-blooded gunman." Knife, fork and spoon tinkled beside the plate.

"Yuh got me wrong, ma'am," he expostulated, between mouthfuls of pie. "I'm jest a poor wandering cow nurse."

"That's why you pack two guns, and shoot the daylights out of Pancho's two fastest gun sharks!" Her tone was cutting. Impulsively, she added, "Say, you're awfully young to be a hired gunman, you can't be much older than I am."

"I ain't hired yet, ma'am."

"You will be—after today."

Bill cleaned up the last crumbs of pie, pushed over his empty plate. "Best pie I ever ate—bring out the rest of it!"

"Hog!"

His lips quirked, he was beginning to like Painted Rock. "And draw a mug of dip f'r yoreself, ma'am, yuh look tuckered out."

She brought half a pie and another cup of coffee, rested her arms on the counter and watched the pie vanish. Bill stirred his coffee, "Who's this Pancho hairpin?"

"Owner of the P/H."

"Gunnin f'r Thompson?"

She raised her shoulders, "They're all gunning for Thompson."

"Thet gent's mighty unpopular."

"Jim Thompson's all right! He came first and grabbed most. Now the have-nots claim it's government range—free for all. Jim doesn't see it that way."

"Why don't they call in the sheriff?"

She sniffed. "We cowmen handle our own whittle-whanging."

"We cowmen!" he mimicked. "Ain't yuh a hasher?"

Fire flashed in the girl's gray eyes. She grabbed the nearest weapon, which chanced to be a long-bladed carving knife, and gripped it in a small, white-knuckled fist. "Another crack like that, Mister Gunman, and I'll settle your hash," she announced ominously.

Bill held both hands high. "Now don't git me wrong, ma'am." His voice was contrite. "My meaning was—yuh ain't no cowman."

Her grip upon the knife handle relaxed, but she eyed him doubtfully. "My father was. Our iron was the TG. When he died, the bank at Deever, that's the county seat, took the spread. Ma just faded away. Jack, that's my brother, was made town marshal and I opened this eating house."

"The fellers must be awful backward around here."

She smiled tightly, "You wouldn't think so, if you ran this joint."

"Ef yuh ain't the most misunderstanin' gal," he grumbled. "Yuh don't crave this hashin' chore, or do yuh?"

"I hate it!" There was bitterness in her intense voice. "But it makes me independent. There are dollars to be made feeding hungry punchers. I'm hoarding money like a squirrel hoards nuts. Some day I'll rod a herd with the TG iron."

"You and me both," he agreed heartily.

"Who asked you to horn in?" she challenged.

"There yuh go—on the prod again! Ain't there room f'r another herd in Arizona?"

"That wasn't the way you put it."

"Wal, thet's the way I meant it," he explained patiently. He left a dollar beside his plate and slid off the stool. "I never craved tuh run in double harness," he threw out casually.

"And I'd sooner hitch up with a sheepherder than a gun wolf," she snapped.

Bill reached for his Stetson, edged toward the door. "Wal, ma'am," he replied gravely, "I've heard tell chance is a mighty fine thing." He ducked fast as his empty platter whizzed through the air and rebounded with a clang off the wall. In the doorway, he paused, eyed the irate redhead and solemnly threw her a kiss. Before she could hurl the cleaver, he was gone.

From habit, Bill awoke at dawn, pulled on his boots, strolled out of the livery barn into the street. Painted Rock still slept. He re-entered the barn, threw the rigging on his pony, and clattered out over the loose boards.

He hit southward, past silent adobes and tumble-down shacks. The frame bungalows of the town's elite, he noticed, lay eastward, in the shadow of the butte.

For a quarter mile, he followed the parallel ruts of the stage road. Then the trail forked, wagon tracks bore westward, where the Black Hills were emerging from the fleeing shadows of night. He followed the wagon tracks.

The sun inched higher, ringed a vagrant cloud with silver and touched the peaks of the distant Dragoons with shining gold. But the rider's mind was on none of these things. Dreamily, he dwelt upon a slim, gray-eyed girl, with a pert nose and freckles.

Spunky as they came, he mused, just like her redheaded brother, the town marshal. It was a miracle some fellow hadn't dropped his rope on her. For the first time, he felt a twinge of regret that he wasn't returning to Painted Rock.

The dun dropped to a walk as the wagon tracks snaked up the flank of a low ridge that bulged out of the plain. So absorbed was the rider with thoughts of argumentative Tess Goodmer that he failed to hear the subdued drumming of hooves on his trail. The menacing whine of a bullet, sharp in the clear morning air, jerked him back to the present. He swung around in the saddle. Not half a mile distant, a bunch of riders were hell-bent in pursuit, quirting their ponies, and overhauling him fast. His quick glance tallied six. Huge black sombreros and glittering silverware plainly marked their identity. They were vaqueros, border desperados. And it looked as though they were out to avenge the shooting of their pards in Painted Rock. Another slug ricocheted from a rock beside him. Yells reached his ears. Bill gave the dun its head and roweled it to a gallop.

Ironshod hooves scattering sand and gravel, the pony leapt forward. The wind whistled through its nostrils as it bounded upward and gained the crest of the ridge. Again Bill swiftly surveyed his pursuers. They were strung along the winding trail, like hounds on the scent. The nearest, forking a big black stallion, was not four hundred paces distant.

He dropped down the ridge, spurring the dun to speed and yet more speed.

The drumming of the black's hooves behind him was plain now. Bent low across the withers of his racing pony, Bill was tempted to loose lead at the yelling vaqueros, now fast closing in, but he held his hand. Good shooting was impossible from the back of a galloping pony and he might need every bullet in his belt later on.

Of a sudden, high sandy walls rose on either side. The ravine quickly narrowed and he pulled his mount down to a trot. The pony rounded a bend and a perpendicular wall faced him—he could go no further. The avenging vaqueros had him cornered as neatly as a wolf in its den.

He swung out of the saddle and trailed his reins. Chest heaving, the pony stood with lowered head, the air whistling through foam-flaked nostrils. Quickly, Bill slid his Winchester out of the boot, left the dun protected from rifleshot by the curve in the canyon, and crunched back over the brittle, sandy earth.

Finally, he bellied down between two huge chunks of rock, and methodically laid out a row of cartridges close to his gun hand. Then he jerked out the makin's and rolled a smoke.

The quiet of death lay on the canyon. Bill peered cautiously from his hideaway and awaited action.

He crushed his cigarette and tautened, cheek cuddling the stock of his rifle. Down canyon, a patch of yellow moved amid the gray boulders and lacy mesquite. Bill squinted through the sunrays that lanced into his eyes, saw that a lithe fellow, resplendently arrayed, was picking his way through the loose rock, making no attempt to seek cover. He held a bright yellow bandana above his head.

"Thet hairpin's hell-bound tuh shake hands with St. Peter," muttered the fugitive, lining the Mexican on his sights. But still the picturesquely garbed rider confidently came on, glancing neither to the right nor left. Soon he was close enough for Bill to distinguish him clearly. His dark features, smooth-shaven except for a tiny mustache, were wreathed in a genial smile.

"Hold it!" barked Bill, when he was twenty paces distant. Only the barrel of the rider's Winchester, his right eye and part of his head were visible as he peered around the base of the rock.

Th dandified Mexican jerked to a stop. If he felt fear, he never showed it. His white teeth flashed in a grin. "*Buenos dias,* señor!" he called. "Why do you hide? I, Pancho Hernandez, am your good fren'."

"Them slugs didn't say so."

Pancho's shoulders rose in a graceful gesture. "Ah, señor, theese vaqueros, they are so imppulsive! I own the P/H, señor. I pay good men like you plenty dinero—mucho more than the Señor Thompson."

"This smells like a lousy trick," thought Bill. "Just as soon as I get from behind this rock his pards will cut me down."

"I ain't f'r hire, Pancho," he said curtly.

Again the Mexican's shoulders rose in an eloquent gesture. "You wear twin guns, señor. You are like the lightning on the draw. You ride into Painted Rock—a stranger. You dreenk weeth Box T gunmen—and you say you are not for hire!"

"Guess I done tied up with Thompson."

The other's teeth flashed. He had a ready smile, and laughing devils danced in his dark eyes. "Mebbe you queet heem, señor. You are trapped—no? We seet down in the shade and wait. You burn up in the sun. Soon you crawl out—we shoot. See, the buzzards are waiting!" He pointed upward. Two of the black scavengers of the desert slow-circled above the canyon. "You weel never see the Boxed T, señor. Come! I pay you mucho dinero."

"I gotta canteen of water," lied Bill, "and plenty shells."

The other calmly rolled a brown-paper cigarette. "I pay two hundred dollair a month and plenty whisky."

"Rattle your hocks! I'm flush and I drink sarsaparilla."

Pancho set a match to his smoke, inhaled with obvious appreciation "*Adios,* señor!" he murmured regretfully. "You are so young—to die."

Bill said nothing, merely moved his gun barrel. The P/H owner turned away, swaggered down canyon.

For a full hour, Bill lay outstretched, alert for action, but nothing moved. The sun edged higher. Its burning rays deflected by the steep walls, converted the canyon into an oven. The trapped rider ran his tongue over parched lips, if only he had filled his canteen!

Soon the mounting sun, flaming white-hot in a brazen bowl, seared his neck and scorched through his shirt. At last, tortured by the sun and inaction, he rose impetuously, determined to attack—three guns crashed almost as one. A slug screamed off the rock, spraying chips into his face. Another lifted his Stetson, a third fanned his cheek. Bill caught a quick flash as the sun glinted on silver, squeezed trigger. A shrill yell of agony cut through the echoing din. Something threshed like a big fish among the boulders. More guns thundered, but Bill chuckled as he bedded down.

The firing died and the echoes muttered away. Again silence clothed the canyon. The hours dragged. Higher and higher climbed the sun. Through the heated air, rocks, walls, stunted shrubs wavered and danced before Bill's bloodshot eyes. His mouth felt as though it was stuffed with cinder's, his body as though he was being slowly grilled. Ants swarmed over him, their sharp nipping like the stabbing of red-hot needles. If he lay still, his rock gave adequate cover, but the slightest movement to either side brought a blast of searching lead.

Some time during those blurred, burning hours of midday he tagged another vaquero.

Then he became aware that the shadow of the big boulder behind him was creeping forward—the sun was dropping. In an hour or two night would cloak the canyon. Then, he knew, his hand would be played out. Covered by darkness, the four remaining vaqueros could creep up unseen and finish him with their knives. He might get one, maybe two, but it was a sure thing they would get him.

CHAPTER FIVE

SHADOWS THICKENED RAPIDLY in the depths of the narrow canyon. Bill emptied his magazine at random into the gloom—and drew a hail of zipping, droning lead. Then, from the height of the wall that towered behind him, a strange gun spoke. The sheltering rock covered his rear, and hid the marksman from the hard-pressed rider, but there was no mistaking the direction of the slugs that whined over his head.

So Pancho had worked behind him! No sooner had this thought entered Bill's head when he became aware of confusion down canyon. He could see nothing in the uncertain light, but shouts of surprise reached his ears, a hoarse yell from a hit vaquero, a confused crashing in the brush. With a joyous uplift of spirit, the trapped man realized that the stranger was blasting his assailants. From the height above, they must have made plain targets. Yelling delirious defiance, Bill flung more shots down canyon. But not a rifle spoke out of the gray murk in reply. Bill eased painfully to his feet, winced at the complaint of cramped muscles, and moved stiffly back to his pony. Unmolested, he rounded the bend, dropped his Winchester back into the saddle boot and stepped up into the saddle. Then he eased through the dusk toward the canyon mouth.

There was no sign of Pancho and the surviving vaqueros. The dun breasted the chaparral that choked the entrance and they emerged into the open. The sun had dropped behind the distant Dragoons, but its waning light was sufficient to reveal four horsemen and two riderless ponies topping the ridge to the east.

For a moment they were silhouetted against the sky, then they dropped down out of sight.

Bill rode out on to the flat, wheeled and searched the benches above the canyon. A rider, astride a piebald, descended the slope. The newcomer was almost atop of Bill before he could distinguish his features beneath the wide-brimmed Stetson. He half expected it would be Fiddlefoot, but this was an older man, clad in the plaid shirt and loose-hanging vest of the range. A faded red bandana was knotted around his neck. Graying hair showed beneath his hat and steely eyes regarded the young rider from beneath sun-bleached eyebrows. His features were desert-eroded, square-cut and his jutting jaw rock-hard. A fighter, and a stayer, registered Bill.

The newcomer pulled rein almost at the young rider's stirrup.

"Thanks, mister!" greeted Bill, and was surprised at the thin, flat croak that emerged from his throat. "I could hear the Pearly Gates creakin'. Yuh got a drink?"

Without a word, the stranger unhooked a canteen from his saddle horn and placed it in Bill's eagerly extended hand. The young rider swallowed lukewarm water, sighed, swallowed again. No bourbon had ever tasted so good. About to tilt the canteen a third time, he hesitated, eyed the heavy-jawed man inquiringly.

"Go ahaid, son," grunted the other. "We got plenty more on the Boxed T." His eyes never left Bill's sun-scorched face.

Finally, the rider stepped down, spilled a little water into the crown of his Stetson and held it to the dun's questing muzzle. Then Bill stretched luxuriously and built a smoke.

"Yuh Bill Carson?" asked the stranger.

"Yuh said it, mister."

"I been huntin' yuh most all day. Fiddlefoot said yuh winged a coupla Pancho's gunnies. Figgered the Mex would lay f'r you, and set my boys combing the hills. Ef it warn't f'r the gunfire I'd never hev located yuh."

"And who might yuh be, mister?"

"Thompson, of the Boxed T."

Cold dismay gripped Bill. Of all the hombres in Grass Valley, Thompson, the man he had sworn to kill, had to ease him out of a tight.

The other man's deep voice broke into his thoughts. "Say, ain't our trails crossed afore?"

"Nope," returned Bill, "yore mebbe thinking of my paw."

"And whar does he hang his hat?"

"In Texas."

Thompson rasped his chin, visibly perplexed.

Bill's fingers fidgeted. Common sense told him that this was the time to cross guns with the cowman. He would never have a better chance to get the job cleaned up and hightail out of Grass Valley. But how could he throw down on a feller who had just risked his life to ease him out of a jack pot?

Thompson spoke again. "Le's ride, Carson. I gamble yore tapeworm's hollerin' and the spread's six-seven miles south."

Still mentally at cross-purposes, Bill swung across his saddle without reply. Side by side, they rode through the gathering darkness.

Bill's first impressions of the Boxed T were dim, starlight did not reveal much to the eye. He saw that the ranch house was a long, one-story rock-and-adobe building, with flat roof and slit windows. Behind it was a bare yard, bounded by a corral and an adobe bunkhouse with a slant-roofed cookshack built against it. Other buildings and corrals loomed in the background.

The pair stepped out of leather at the water trough in the yard. Cigarette tips glowed like red sparks all around, as riders hunkered against the buildings, enjoying their smokes after the heat of the day. A tall form stalked toward them. "Wal," rumbled Fiddlefoot, "so yuh done dropped a rope on the maverick, Jim. I figgered he was totin' a harp."

"He most was," grunted Thompson. "Git him a bunk and some chow. The hairpin's been trading lead with Pancho's coyotes. I'll handle the hosses."

Bedroll balanced upon his shoulder, Bill followed Fiddlefoot across the hoof-chopped yard. A lamp flamed yellow in the adobe bunkhouse, set on a table around which the inevitable group of card players were gathered. Two tiers of bunks ran along each side. Most, Bill noticed, were in use.

Fiddlefoot indicated a lower bunk near the door. "Feller drew his time this forenoon," he explained, "so I nailed it down f'r you." He folded up like a jointed rule and watched Bill alertly as the young rider loosened the knots on his roll. "Now gimme the low-down on Pancho!"

Bill told of the fracas in the canyon.

Fiddlefoot roared in delight. "Ef yuh ain't the doggonest wildcat thet ever clawed Grass Valley! Wal, let's hit up the dough puncher f'r chow!"

The beanstalk left Bill in the cookshack, after persuading Pegleg, an alkalied old cook with a lurid vocabularly and a stiff leg, to set out a well-filled platter of leftovers and a mug of hot coffee. "I gotta wise up the boys about Pancho," explained Fiddlefoot. "Four Mexicans in two days! Ef thet don't beat hell!"

Bill was delving into the victuals like a hungry horse when the cookshack door slammed open and a big rangy man banged in. Pete Lastro, *caporal* of the Boxed T, might have shone in a brawl but not in a beauty contest. His hawklike face was tanned the color of mahogany and his long nose had been broken and twisted askew in some past fracas. Thick black eyebrows met above his sharp eyes, which now scanned Bill's youthful form with cold bleakness. A gunbelt sagged beneath his sleeveless leather vest and his spurs had small rowels.

Bill was busy. He glanced up and eyed the visitor casually, then forked another mouthful of beans. The cook suddenly became engrossed in sorting knives and forks by the sink.

"Ain't I sed—no handouts in the cookshack?" rasped the foreman.

"Boss sent him over, Pete. He jest rode in." Pegleg rattled tinware nervously.

Hands on his hips, the big foreman stood in the doorway, eyes dwelling distastefully upon Bill. "Another lily-fingered gun shark!" There was a venomous bite in his voice. "Fit f'r nothing but tuh set around, wolf good chow and gamble. From now on—yuh—eat with the crew and keep outa the cookhouse."

Bill pushed away his empty plate, drained his mug. He felt better now. His chair scraped back. He hitched up his gunbelt and gave the foreman full attention. "And who might yuh be, mister?"

"Yore boss!"

The blue-eyed rider smiled, a slow, provoking smile. He didn't like the crooked-nosed man and it was plain the foreman felt the same way about him. He patted the butt of his right-hand gun, "I make talk with thus, mister, and I gamble I kin talk faster'n you."

Pegleg swung around with a quick gasp of surprise. This was fight talk and no one spoke back to Pete Lastro—twice.

For moments tight silence held the shack. And then the foreman suddenly flung around and the cookhouse door slammed behind him.

"B'gawd!" ejaculated Pegleg. "Fust time I ever see Pete sidestep. Yuh watch yore step, young feller—he won't ferget. Heah, lemme fill yore mug!"

But Bill Carson had more on his mind than the ornery foreman of the Boxed T. One thought weighed him down like a ten-ton rock—paw had sent him to Arizona to do a job, and that job had to be done. The longer he put it off, the more unpleasant it would become. He was conscious of a liking, a growing admiration, for tough Jim Thompson. The hard-bitten cowman was playing a lone hand against the Valley. And if it wasn't for Thompson, mused Bill somberly, the coyotes right now would be tearing the flesh off his bones. Then he visioned his father, with two useless legs, crippled for life, warped in mind and body by a slug from Thompson's gun—in the back. It was squarely up to him—Bill Carson—to even the score.

Morosely, the troubled rider emptied his mug of coffee, nodded thanks to the cook, wandered outside and hunkered against the wall of the cookshack. The yard was dark and deserted now. From the bunkhouse behind him came the brisk plunk-plunk of Fiddlefoot's banjo, gusts of loud laughter and the stamp of high-heeled boots. Through the din rose Fiddlefoot's voice singing and singing.

The chorus, that told of a pretty gal, recalled a little eating house in Painted Rock and a girl with coppery hair. Envy stirred the lonely man, hunched in the gloom, envy of those carefree punchers whooping it up in the bunkhouse. They had no blood feuds to burden their minds. Right then, he would have given his right arm to change places with any one of them.

To his front, broad bars of light marked the slit windows of the ranch house. Through one, he glimpsed Thompson, seated at a roll-top desk, working on his books. The easy way, considered Bill, would be to get the cowman from the obscurity of the yard, ditch the gun and mingle with the crew when they poured out of the bunkhouse. No one could pin it on him. But he knew, deep in his heart, that he could never kill that way.

Wearily, he hunched lower and sucked a cold cigarette. The bunkhouse shook beneath the impact of stomping boots and loud singing.

With an abrupt gesture, the forlorn rider spat out the sodden remnants of his cigarette and jerked to his feet. Hell, why chew on it, get the chore over, quicker the better.

He jingled across the yard. The ponies in the corral were botched shadows. He squeezed between the rails, coiled rope in hand. The nearest ponies eyed him with a questioning flip of the ears and moved away. He whistled, a long, low note. The dun drifted up.

Bill steered his mount toward the pole gate, lowered it and led the animal outside. He was casting around for his saddle when a burly form bulged out of the darkness.

"Ridin'—Carson?" grated the foreman's voice.

Mentally, Bill cursed his luck.

"Nope," he returned shortly. "The dun's saddle-galled. Yuh got any dope around here?"

"Take a looksee in the barn." Lastro turned and crunched away.

"I gamble he's keeping cases on me," thought Bill. " 'Pears like I can kiss my chance of a fast getaway good night." He slipped a hackamore on the dun and knotted it loosely around a rail. Located his saddle. Draped a folded blanket across the pony's back, softy set the saddle in place and tightened the cinches. Then peered around, seeking the foreman. But Lastro had disappeared. He slipped on the bridle and the pony was readied.

Stubbornly, with dragging feet and set features, Bill headed for the house. The tempo from the bunkhouse had changed. Fiddlefoot's banjo plunked dolefully and the deep-voiced chant of the crew welled into the night:

"Oh, bury me not on the lone prair-e-e
Where the coyotes howl and the winds blow free;
Oh, bury me not on the lone prair-e-e
In a narrow grave, jest six by three."

To the plodding Bill, it was a dirge of fate. It seemed like the whole danged spread was wise to him—a lousy coyote out to beef the man who saved his life.

A door in the rear of the house yawned wide open. Bill stepped into an unlighted kitchen, crossed it and emerged into a wide passageway. Doors opened off on either side. At its end, light flooded through a doorway and Thompson was in plain sight, bent over the desk, only his broad back visible.

It seemed to the slow-pacing Bill that he could hear Crawler's venomed voice: "Git him now, git him in the spine, like he got me! And you kin make your getaway faster." But he held his arms stiff and moved on, on, down the seemingly endless length of the wide passage.

At sound of jingling spurs, the cowman straightened in his chair, his head came around. He recognized Bill, as the young rider stepped out of the gloom of the unlighted passageway and moved through the doorway. His leathery features creased in a welcoming grin, "Howdy! Heah, Milly, meet Bill Carson, fastest gunhand in the Valley. He tagged four of Pancho's chili-eaters already."

Startled, Bill's glance searched to right and left, saw that a girl was sitting quietly by the glassless slit window. He drew a quick breath of surprise.

"My gal!" drawled Thompson. She merely nodded brusquely and measured Bill with eyes in which disapproval was plain. Her face was oval, with more than a hint of stubbornness in her rounded chin. Clustered in thick ringlets, her fluffy blonde hair reminded Bill of spun gold. There was an imperious set to her small chin and a querulousness about her red lips that warned him she was high-strung and unbridled. A spoilt kid, he thought. A mannish gray shirt and overalls seemed to add to rather than detract from her femininity.

At Bill's muttered greeting, a quick frown creased her tanned forehead.

"You seem young to be a hardened gunman, Mr. Carson!"

"Gunnies never grow old, gal," chuckled Thompson. "Pancho's boys almost handed him a harp this P.M.

Her eyes dropped to the thonged-down guns. "Ugh!" she shuddered, "I wonder the ghosts of the men you kill don't haunt you. Good night!"

With that, she rose and coldly shouldered past him, out of the room.

"Don't let Milly faze yuh," advised Thompson, good-naturedly. "She don't take kindly tuh the Boxed T hirin' gun-hands, and she sure lays her cards down, face up." He opened a drawer of the desk, extended a box of cigars to his visitor.

"Nope," said Bill shortly, "I roll 'em."

The tone of his voice brought a quick, questioning glance from the cowman.

"What's eatin' yuh?" he inquired, selected a cigar, bit off the end and leaned back in his chair.

"Plenty!" Bill glanced quickly behind him. The girl had gone, half closing the door after her. "Yuh wouldn't know me, Thompson, but mebbee yuh recollect pluggin' my paw in the back." The cowman touched a match to his cigar, shook his head in negation, eyes alert.

"Yuh should—yuh crippled him, with a slug in the spine." Bill's voice was tight with growing anger.

"Mebbe, son," agreed Thompson mildly. "Reckon I matched cutters with plenty men in my day."

His accuser was half crouched now, crooked fingers poised above his guns, slitted eyes following the older man's every movement.

"Wal, yuh crippled paw—from behind—and he sent me tuh git yuh. Jerk yore iron, Thompson!" Bill threw the words like bullets, from between tight lips.

But the old cowman continued to draw placidly upon his cigar, eying the menacing figure of his challenger with unmoved features. "So yore ribbing tuh plug me, son?" he said quietly.

"Yuh bet yore life I am," raged Bill. "Go f'r yore iron, yuh dirty bushwhacker, or I'll gut-shoot yuh—pronto." His right hand fastened upon the smooth butt of a gun.

"Son," came back Thompson, unruffled, "I could no more bushwhack yore paw than yuh could shoot a man who wouldn't draw. Take the weight off yore laigs. Set down! Le's hash this over."

"Jerk yore gun!" choked Bill. His shirt was wet against his back.

"When did I git yore paw?"

"Twenty years back or more."

"Thet's a long time tuh carry a grudge."

"He had to carry it, till I could—his legs was crippled."

"Yuh dead sure yuh got the righ hombre?"

"Plumb certain!" Bill's fingers tightened spasmodically upon the gun butt. "Cut the palaver and draw—gordamn yuh!"

Face still expressionless, Thompson shook his head, thumbs hooked carelessly in his leather belt.

"Then, blast yuh, Thompson, I'm comin' asmokin'." The starkness of desperation rang in the younger man's hoarse voice. His right-hand gun blurred up and out.

CHAPTER SIX

NOT A NERVE TWITCHED upon Jim Thompson's rugged features as the hammer of Bill's .44 snapped back and the long barrel lined on his hairy chest.

Two pairs of eyes met across the adobe-walled office—the cowman's calm as deep pools; Bill Carson's glowing like molten glass. Death's spectral finger was poised to touch Thompson's shirted shoulder.

A curse that was almost a groan ripped from Bill's taut lips. The pointing barrel dropped. "Damn yore guts, Thompson, I can't blast yuh thisaway!"

"Yuh'd be tarnation sorry, son."

"Sorry!" flamed the other. "Ain't yuh got it comin'? I'll call yuh out before the crew, b'gawd, where you can't side-step without showin' yore yeller to the brisket bone. I'll git yuh!"

He dropped the gun back into its holster, backed to the door, swung around and pushed blindly into the darkened passage—and plunged headlong into a bulky figure standing silent in the shadow.

Bill jerked to a stop, as the stranger reeled before the impact. By the lamplight, streaming through the doorway behind him, he recognized the twisted nose and hawklike features of Pete Lastro, the Boxed T foreman. Panting, he glared at the big man, then pushed past him and hastened down the passageway.

Two questions hammered in his head—how long had Lastro been standing outside the door and why hadn't he pulled his gun when Thompson was threatened? "Maybe," reasoned Bill savagely, "he was waitin' for me to beef Thompson, then he would have got me in the back and grabbed the Box T for himself."

Over in the bunkhouse, Fiddlefoot had the boys stomping and roaring again.

Bill crossed the yard and stripped the gear off his pony, mentally scourging himself. One hell of a mess he had made of things. Acted worse than a schoolmarm. Thompson had bluffed him through cold nerve, had dared him to shoot and he didn't have enough sand in his craw to loose the hammer. Now that crooked-nosed foreman was wise and he'd have to watch the pair of them.

Bill hazed his mount into the corral again, leaned in disgust against the rails, scowling at the twinkling stars.

A full hour passed before he hit for the bunkhouse. He had seen the foreman's shadowy outline emerge from the house and cross the yard. Light still streamed from the slit windows of Thompson's office. Finally, the banjo was silent and the singing died down. Bill waited a spell and then headed for his bunk. His mood was more akin to murder than merriment.

When he stepped through the bunkhouse door there was no sound in the room save the deep breathing of sleeping men.

Bill unstrapped his spurs, yanked off his boots and slid between the soogans, but it was long before he sank into uneasy slumber. Bathed in sweat, he twisted in a delirium of nightmare. Now the foam-flecked jaw of a wolf fastened upon his shoulder. Helpless, he writhed and struggled, but the fangs only sank the deeper. Then he was roughly shaken awake and hauled out of his bunk. Half awake, he blinked around in the cold light of dawn. Bleak faces ringed him and he became aware that the foreman's gnarled fingers were digging into his right shoulder.

He slammed a left hook into Lastro's ribs before a puncher fastened on to his free arm. Wide awake now, he glared up into the foreman's rough-hewn features. "What's eatin yuh?" he demanded irately.

"Plenty!" growled Lastro. "How come yuh knifed the boss?"

"Yore loco!"

The foreman's grasp tightened. "Yuh can't shuffle outa this. Last night I heard yuh swear yuh'd git Jim, over in the office. Yuh saddled yore pony f'r a quick getaway. Wal, he's layin' in his office right now with a knife in his back. And yuh stuck him, yuh mangy gun-totin' skunk!"

With a quick twist, Bill broke free, hurled himself at the foreman. A dozen hands grabbed at him, wrenched him back, held him gasping.

"Boss daid, Pete?" inquired a hard-breathing puncher.

"Mighty close tuh it. Cherokee lit for town tuh git the sawbones. Anyways," the foreman eyed Bill's disheveled figure grimly, "I reckon we'll string up this rat, pronto." A deep, rumbling growl of approval arose.

"Lissen!" pleaded the prisoner. "Ef I'd knifed Thompson, I'd have beat it. Yuh got the wrong feller."

"Sure!" mocked Lastro. "Yuh acted slick, too danged slick. Figgered yuh'd bluff it out. Nope, Carson, yuh tangled yore spurs—f'r the last time."

Bill remained silent. Protest, he knew, was waste of words. Well, he thought in resignation, paw was avenged, anyway.

"Le's go!" rasped the foreman. He led the way outside into the gray half-light. Hatless and in his socks, Bill was hustled behind him in the center of a knot of hard-eyed punchers. After them straggled the rest of the crew.

Hopelessly, the condemned man glanced around the yard. He didn't have a pard on the spread, except Fiddlefoot, and he'd never been overly friendly with the tall rider. But even Fiddlefoot had disappeared. Bill's stomach coiled into a cold, hard knot at the thought of choking to death at the end of a rope. But his captors gave him little time for thought. Relentlessly, hard hands pushed him ahead.

Silently, except for the jingling of spurred boots, they led him toward the big horse barn. At last he caught sight of Fiddlefoot's tall form, half bent, casting around outside the office window.

Looked like the stringy rider had pulled out of trouble, thought Bill. Couldn't blame him. They had ridden into Painted Rock together and in its present ugly mood, the crew might feel an impulse to string him up, too.

The knot of men clumped into the semidarkness of the barn. Bill glanced upward. Massive beams ran from side to side, ten feet above his head. While they held him, a puncher shook out his rope, made an upward cast. The rope sailed neatly across a beam, dropped down and swung pendulumlike, just above Bill's bare head. The puncher shook the loop down, until it lay slack, itching against the prisoner's back.

There was momentary hesitation among the cold-eyed group. No one seemed anxious to set the noose around Bill's neck. With a growl of impatience; Lastro elbowed forward, grabbed the dangling rope.

Jaw clamped tight, eyes stoical, Bill waited for the end.

As Lastro dropped the loop over his head, he heard a quick step in the rear. The foreman was roughly shouldered against him and the threatening noose flicked off.

"You hairpins loco, swingin' Bill Carson?" It was Fiddlefoot's deep voice, heavy with anger.

Lastro swung around to face the tall rider, eyes baleful. "Keep outa this," he growled, "or I'll knock yore ears down tuh where yuh kin use 'em f'r wings. We gotta job tuh do."

"Not when I'm around!" Fiddlefoot was behind the prisoner, but from the startled expression that leapt into the foreman's eyes, Bill knew that the tall man had jerked a gun.

The punchers pressed closer, in ominous silence. "This coyote knifed the boss, better drift along, Fiddlefoot!" threw in one harshly.

"Hawgwash!" snorted the bean pole. "The jasper who knifed Jim Thompson was a Mexican with small feet."

"Yeah! Squint-eyed, with curly hair!" sneered Lastro. "Go plunk yore banjo, yuh ain't easin' yore pard outa this."

"Button up!" advised Fiddlefoot shortly. "Now lissen, you hammerheads, there's sign outside of Jim's winder, the tracks are plain. What's more, the killer left this behind." He held up a large brass button, of a type that usually ornamented vaqueros' velvet jackets.

The crew was all attention now. Eyes left the prisoner and focused upon Fiddlefoot's bony face. Only the foreman was unimpressed. "Beat it, bean pole, or we'll hist you up, too," he threatened. "Hell, fellers, this jasper's runnin' a sandy. Ain't he Carson's pard?"

For the first time, there was dissension among the crew. The small group of hired gunhands stood apart; from them came growls of angry disagreement. There was little intermingling between the gunmen and the regular cow hands, and the gunnies counted Fiddlefoot and Bill as their kind.

The tall rider laughed silently, his deep-set eyes weighing Lastro. "So my tongue's crooked! Wal, go see Jim Thompson, he ain't checked out yet. Mebbe yuh'll take his word."

The foreman hesitated, noting that the tight group of gunmen was loosening as they shuffled apart, leaving each a clear field of fire. It was plain that hanging Bill Carson, after Fiddlefoot's challenge, would be the signal for a bloody fracas. "Wal," he came back grudgingly, "ef Jim clears the jasper—hunkydory! But ef he don't, the lobo swings, and swings high."

Again Bill was hauled outside and returned to the bunkhouse. Here he was released and left under the guard of two alert waddies. He pulled on his boots and looked around for his guns, but they had disappeared.

The sun rose behind the silent ranch house, its rays flooding through the bunkhouse door. Lastro had set the crew busy around the spread, except for the waddies guarding Bill and half a dozen gunhands, who bunched around the table and embarked upon a listless fame of stud. The gunmen had sided him in the Painted Rock fracas, considered Bill, and backed Fiddlefoot in the barn, but right now he might have ceased to exist, for all the attention they gave him.

Apathetically, he hunkered by his bunk and smoked endless cigarettes. His fate hung on Thompson's word, and it was a sure thing that a man who would put a bullet in his paw's spine would not save him from the rope. All the more so, after he had threatened to shoot the cowman on sight.

Cards slapped drearily on the table, coin clinked, talk droned. Bill glanced toward the players and met the blank stare of a wizened gunman. The other's right eyelid dropped, his gaze shifted to the bunk behind the prisoner, then returned to the tables as he gathered up his hand.

For the first time Bill felt a faint stir of hope, Fiddlefoot wasn't the only well-wisher he had around. But why did the wizened gunnie stare at the bunk?

Leisurely, he rose, stretched and sprawled on the bunk. A thrill shot through him—the hard metal of a six gun, hidden between the soogans, pressed against the small of his back. Before he had a chance to ease it out, unobserved by the two guards, Lastro's burly form blocked the doorway.

"Boss craves tuh talk with yuh, Carson," he grated. "Try and make a break and I'll bore yuh."

Dogged by the foreman, Bill crossed the yard. A buggy was drawn up by the house and, as the pair approached, a short, roly-poly man in townsman's garb, toting a black bag, trotted out of the back door.

Lastro steered his prisoner down the corridor, knuckled a closed door. Mildred Thompson, face agitated and eyes reddened, opened it and motioned them inside.

The rancher lay upon a brass bedstead, only his head visible above the covers. His square face was haggard and blanched beneath the tan, and there was pain in his blue eyes. He motioned Bill to step close. "Stick around outside, Pete," he told the foreman in a husky whisper. "I wanna powwow with Carson."

Lastro dragged his feet, eyeing Bill uncertainly. The girl took his arm; her fingers shook with nervous tension. "Please!" she said brokenly. Muttering protest, the foreman moved out into the corridor.

The old cowman's features creased with grim amusement as he gazed up into Bill's unshaven, scowling face. "So the boys most strung yuh up f'r knifin me!" he croaked. "I reckon they would swing yuh right now, ef I give the word."

"I don't use a knife and I'm no bushwhacker," said Bill.

"Mebbe, son, but some yeller bustard got me from behind, and yuh warn't exactly friendly."

"I ain't friendly right now," retorted the rider.

"Stubborn as a Missouri mule!" chuckled the wounded man. "Wal, here's the deal—I'm outa business f'r two-three months, accordin' to Doc Blaine. Most all the juice is drained outa me. The Boxed T is pressed hard. They got me ringed like a calf in a pack of coyotes, but this calf packs a kick. Yuh take over till I git back on my feet and I'll swear a greaser knifed me. Yuh buck—and yuh hang. I reckon thet's plain!"

His head dropped back on the pillow and he lay slack, exhausted.

"I can't figger yore play, mister," Bill's voice mirrored his perplexity. "Yuh know I hate yore guts and yet yuh ask me tuh take over. Yuh *must* be loco. Ain't Peter Lastro foreman?"

"Pete's got no more brains than a bull, and mebbe I ain't so loco."

"Aw, to hell with the Boxed T!" burst out Bill impulsively.

"Yuh won't be around tuh see it go to hell!"

The door eased open and Fiddlefoot ducked to clear the frame. He crossed the room with long strides. "Doc said yuh gotta rest, Jim!"

"Ain't I restin'?"

Bill turned appealingly to the tall rider. "Lissen! He wants me tuh rod the Boxed T—or swing. He must be crazy!"

Fiddlefoot grinned. "Crazy like a coyote!"

"It don't make sense!"

"I'd sure hate tuh swing."

"But yuh found tracks and—" There was no mirth in Fiddlefoot's eyes as they met the prisoner's troubled gaze. "I was lyin', Bill. Hadda stall thet necktie party. Ef Jim claims yuh knifed him—yuh shore did."

"And yuh'd let me hang?"

"I reckon so," said Fiddlefoot coldly.

" 'Pears like you jaspers hold all the aces," declared Bill bitterly. "Wal, I'll throw my hand in. I'll run the doggoned spread, though paw u'l cuss me to his dying day. But when wuh git around, Thompson, there's gonna be a showdown."

The wounded cowman and Fiddlefoot exchanged glances.

"Yuh swear yuh'll put yore weight behind the job, son?" There was an unfamiliar note of appeal in Thompson's weak voice.

"I'll give it all I got, damn yuh!"

The cowman glanced at Fiddlefoot, his eyes bright. "Round up Bill, Dakota, Slim, Baldy and Tex. Bring 'em in with Pete. I'm gonna give 'em the low-down on their new boss. Set down, son, and rest yore laigs."

CHAPTER SEVEN

BILL ALMOST FORGOT HIS TROUBLES at sight of the utter bewilderment reflected on the weathered features of Pete Lastro and the Boxed T old-timers, packed into Jim Thompson's bedroom, when the cowman broke the news. The youth they had almost hanged an hour before was now their boss!

Before their spluttering objection boiled into violent protest Fiddlefoot had firmly shooed them outside again, with an indignant reminder that Doc Blaine had prescribed complete quiet for the wounded man.

In heated confab, they gathered around Lastro in the yard, while Bill made a beeline for the bunkhouse. His first thought was for his guns. He found them in the foreman's bunk and buckled them on with deep satisfaction. Chances were he'd be needing them before long.

The news flamed over the spread faster than a brush fire. Men converged upon the ground around Lastro like bees drawn to a mess of molasses—and buzzed as busily. The hired gunhands still fingered the pasteboards around the bunkhouse table, with stolid indifference. They were not interested in who was kingpin of the Boxed T as long as he paid regular.

Bill hunkered by the bunkhouse door. His head was still awhirl. If paw ever got word of what had happened, he reflected, he'd be so doggoned riled he'd crawl to Arizona, dragging a shotgun behind him. Crawler had sent him to rub out Thompson and here he was easing the cowman out of a tight.

The crush of punchers broke up. Lastro entered the house and a dozen or more riders headed for their bunks. They passed their newly made boss without a glance and jammed through the bunkhouse doorway. One by one, they came out again, toting their spooled bedrolls, and trudged toward the corral. Dust rose as they dropped loops upon their ponies. It was plain that they were through with the Boxed T. A good third of the crew gone already, thought Bill wryly. Barring a miracle, the Boxed T was washed up.

Fiddlefoot's tall form towered beside the gloomy-eyed Bill. He sank down on his heels beside the new boss. "Lastro sure cut out a slice of the saddle stock," he drawled, indicating the milling bunch of men and horses around the corral gate.

"Let 'em quit!" grunted Bill. "We'll have trouble aplenty without troublemakers. What I can't figger is why Thompson wished this doggone job on me."

"Jim acts surprisin' sometimes."

"Yuh act like yore well acquainted."

"Knowed him on and off f'r twenty years or more," returned Fiddlefoot carelessly. Bill's thoughts flew back to the night he rode into the lanky rider's camp. The recollection was plain, Fiddlefoot had said he'd never met Jim Thompson. Why had he lied? Bill decided to chew on the problem for a while and casually switched the subject, "Don't they draw time around here?"

"Yep, Lastro's collectin' f'r the bunch, inside. Thompson's gal keeps the books and handles the dinero. But Jim said tuh tell yuh the office is yores, any time yuh want tuh use it, and yuh kin draw on the bank at Painted Rock f'r reasonable expenses."

In a compact bunch, the quitters clattered by, rolls tied behind their saddles, big Pete Lastro at their head. As his pony jogged past, the foreman spat derisively into the dust, almost at Bill's feet, but the young rider hunkered stolidly, face unmoved.

"Jest beggin' f'r trouble," rumbled Fiddlefoot.

"He'll get it," promised Bill curtly, "when he ain't got a bunch at his back. Le's give the office a once-over!"

The manner of Jim Thompson's knifing was plain, pointed out Bill, as they stood in the plainly furnished room that served as ranch office and eyed the irregular brown blotch on the beaten earth floor where the cowman's blood had drained away. In the lamplight he made a plain target, while his assailant was hidden by the darkness outside. His broad back presented an easy mark. A thrown knife was silent, where a gunshot would have aroused the spread.

"My guess is Pancho," said Bill to Fiddlefoot. His roving glance ran over the rough walls, focused upon a framed reward notice, yellowed and spotted with age, hung above the desk. He could have sworn it was not there the night before. Curious, he stepped closer. Behind him, Fiddlefoot followed every move. Bill's pulse quickened. There was a curious familiarity about the crude reproduction of the wanted man's features. Quickly, he read:

$5,000 REWARD
Dead or Alive
WANTED FOR MURDER

Jules Lefevre, alias Lightning Lefevre. Height 5' 10"; weight about 160 lb. Hair black, eyes dark. Wanted for holdup of Laramine County Bank and murder of James Goldman, cashier; holdup of Cattlemen's Bank, Lennox, and killing of George White, deputy sheriff. Holdup of Custer Bank, with violence. Also for looting gold and greenbacks exceeding $80,000 in value. Other charges pending. Dangerous gunman. A reward of 25% will also be paid for all loot recovered.

J. Thompson, Sheriff
Laramine County, Texas.

The yellowed sheet bore a date twenty-seven years back. Heart hammering, Bill stood still as a statue as the implications of the tersely worded notice sank in. Paw was a bandit and a killer—and he was the son of a renegade. Jim Thompson had rodded the law before he moved to Arizona. Then the musing youth remembered Fiddlefoot, standing silent behind him. So this was the real reason the tall rider was anxious to locate Crawler—$5,000 reward and 25% cut if he could nose out that $90,000 loot.

With an effort Bill regained composure. "So thet's the hombre yuh was yawping about first time we met up," he commented casually.

"Thet's the rattlesnake," rumbled Fiddlefoot. "Crippled my gun hand in the Laramine Bank fracas. The bustard could sure handle an iron. Yuh plumb certain yuh ain't crossed his trail?"

Bill pointed to the date on the notice. "Use yore conk; I warn't even foaled them days."

"Lefevre pulled plenty jobs after thet. I gotta hunch he's above ground yet."

"And I gamble he was planted years back."

"Would yuh bet on it?" There was subtle mockery in Fiddlefoot's dry tones.

"I never bet on a sure thing," returned Bill indifferently. "Say, lookat them cowpokes, settin' around like a flock of broody hens." He nodded at the lounging punchers in the yard, plain through the slit window. "What say yuh keep 'em busy. Yore foreman!"

When Fiddlefoot left the office, he turned to the reward notice again. It was paw, no mistake about that. Many things became plain now—why pouched gold was heaped in the trunk beside paw's bed. And he'd always thought it was Crawler's hard-earned savings! Why Lightning Lefevre became Crawler Carson. And why Crawler let it be known that anyone who stuck his nose into Panther Gulch would be greeted with lead.

He dropped into Thompson's swivel chair, eyes still fixed on the damning proof of his paw's lawlessness. What would Jim Thompson say, he wondered with grim humor, if he knew he had saved the son of Lightning Lefevre from the rope and made him ramrod of the Boxed T?

Well, the blue-eyed rider determined savagely, he might be a no-good son of a gun, with a murderer for father and heaven alone knew who for mother, but he'd show Jim Thompson he could carry out his end of a bargain.

Again his eyes dropped in moody introspection. The picture of Lightning Lefevre, snarling from the faded reward notice, drew them back like a magnet. It seemed to taunt him, a virulent, unclean thing. In a quick spasm of anger he reached up, wrenched the frame off the wall, flung it down and ground it beneath the sharp heel of his riding boot into a mash of torn paper and splintered wood. Then he savagely kicked the remnants beneath the desk. God, if a man could only pick his parents!

Quick steps tapped in the passage outside. Bill swiftly composed his features. Milly Thompson hurried in, sighted his still figure, hesitated, then brushed past him to the desk. There was no mistaking the hostility in her eyes.

She rolled up the sliding top that shielded the desk, glanced quickly over several account books, neatly stacked inside, banged the top down again.

"I handle the books—and the money—on this ranch," she said meaningfully.

"Yore welcome tuh the chore, ma'am. How's yore paw doin'?"

"As well as we can expect."

She bit her underlip, abruptly faced him. "Why did dad appoint you, a stranger, to take his place on the Boxed T?"

Bill shrugged, his lips twisting with amusement at the indignation in her clear voice. "Yore guess is as good as mine, ma'am."

Her smooth forehead creased into fine lines of distaste. "You, of all men! Young—and wild. Just a paid killer!"

"Yep, I'm all that," he agreed readily. "I guess yuh want tuh help yore paw?"

"Of course!" Her eyebrows went up.

"Wal, what say yuh give me a hand tuh save the spread?"

"The best way to save the spread is not to fight—it's hopeless to battle the whole Valley."

"Yuh and me don't think alike, ma'am," he said roughly. "Jest what are we up agenst?"

"Every spread in Grass Valley."

"How many spreads and how many guns?"

"Too many! Why don't you compromise, Mr. Carson?" Her tone was more friendly now. "Here, let me draw you a map!" She turned to the desk again, pushed up the sliding cover and laid a sheet of notepaper upon the flat top. Rapidly, she sketched a rough map of Grass Valley, indicating the various ranches.

Bill watched over her shoulder, admiring the skill and certainty of her slim fingers. She looked back and her golden hair brushed his cheek. "Well, is that plain?"

"How many men?" he prompted.

Quickly, she jotted down:

Circle S	14
P/H	12
Rocking T	8
Lazy M	10
Frying Pan	6
Nesters	12
	62

"That's a guess," she admitted, "there are probably more; nesters have been getting quite thick in the Black Hills."

"Jehoshaphat!" muttered Bill. "Thet's long odds. How many we got?"

"We had thirty-four on the pay roll, but Pete and ten other men drew their time this morning, which leaves twenty-three."

"Hell!" he ejaculated.

"Don't you think we had better quit?" she urged. "What else can we expect but defeat. Think of the killing and suffering you can avoid—all to no purpose. Let me pay off those gunmen and I'll tell dad you've decided it's foolish to fight!"

Would Tess Goodmer talk that way? wondered Bill. Aloud he said, "Hold yore hosses, ma'am! I ain't quittin'. Mebbe we kin whittle 'em down."

"And maybe you'll be whittled down—to size," she came back disdainfully. With a challenging toss of her gleaming hair, she turned away, every heeltap telegraphing angry disapproval.

Thinking hard, Bill stared out of the slit window across the sun-swept yard. Twenty-three men against sixty-two, and the enemies of the Boxed T ringed him, ready to leap in and slash from any direction. There were plenty cows out there, Thompson's beef, and it was his job to guard them. How? There was only one answer—more men.

He glimpsed Fiddlefoot's stringy length by the blacksmith shop. Folding the map of the Valley, he slipped it into a vest pocket, then hurried out of the house.

"We need more gunhands!" he told the tall rider, shortly.

"I need more dinero," grunted Fiddlefoot, "but there don't seem much around."

"Kin I pick up any gun slicks in Painted Rock?"

"Every jasper who kin heft a gun in Grass Valley has been hired."

"Ain't there more cow towns around?"

"Nearest is Deever, the county seat. Yuh go yellin f'r gunhands around Deever and the sheriff u'll horn in, pronto."

"Gordamn it!" burst out Bill in exasperation. "Ain't yuh got nothin' tuh offer?"

Fiddlefoot directed a slow stream of tobacco juice at a darting lizard. "Sure," he rumbled, "I figger yuh done bit off more'n yuh kin chew."

"F'r yore size," Bill came back tartly, "you pack less brains than anything I've met up with outside of burros." With this parting shot, he swung away and headed for the corral.

Fiddlefoot rolled a smoke with his left hand and followed the course of his chunky boss as he angrily scuffed dust across the yard. The tall man shook with inward merriment.

Fiddlefoot still stood in the shade of the blacksmith shop when Bill rode out.

"Yuh ain't quittin'—boss?" he inquired dryly.

"Quittin'! I'm gonna get me some men, if I have tuh rope and hog-tie the hombres tuh bring 'em in."

Fiddlefoot stood in the corridor of the ranch house. He gazed around guiltily, saw no sign of Mildred, knuckled Jim Thompson's door softly and eased in. The cowman's eyes, deep in his square features, sought him eagerly. "Wal, how's the maverick makin' out?" he inquired huskily.

The new foreman settled his long length on a chair beside the bed and chuckled. "Mad enough tuh bite hisself. Right now he jest helled off tuh git him some more men. I done told him there warn't a gun f'r hire in Grass Valley, but did it faze him—not on yore life!"

"I'll lay a ten-spot agenst a beer check he rounds up a passel," challenged the wounded cowman.

"Doggone it, Jim, there ain't a gunhand loose within fifty miles, and ef there was he wouldn't tie up with the Boxed T—not in the jam we're in."

"The bet still stands!"

"Yuh'd lay yore last dollar on thet little rooster!" accused the lanky rider.

"I shore would," returned Jim Thompson complacently.

CHAPTER EIGHT

LIKE A HUGE BRONZE SNAKE, lazily gliding across the Valley, Lost River looped out of the Black Hills and coiled across the flats, dividing Boxed T range neatly in half. At Painted Rock the shallow stream swung south, wandered aimlessly toward the Border, shrank into a succession of mudholes and finally was sucked up entirely by the thirsty desert.

The wagon road that linked Jim Thompson's spread with town straddled the river five miles northeast of the ranch.

Still unfamiliar with the terrain, Bill followed the wagon tracks. Far ahead, the blue bulk of Painted Rock was square-set against the horizon; westward, sullen and shimmering through rising heat waves, the Black Hills undulated against the backdrop of the distant Dragoons. Across his front ran a wavering line of gaunt cottonwoods, towering above the chaparral that marked the course of the river. It was as hot as the backlog of hell, admitted Bill, and only a prime jackass, such as himself, would hit the trail in the heat of noon.

Gleaming like molten metal, bordered with verdant green brush, abounding with leafy shade, the river was balm to his sun-seared eyes. Right then he decided to cease acting like a jackass. He would laze awhile by the lapping water and drift into Painted Rock in the cool of evening. And such are the devious ways of fate, that in so doing he signed the death warrants of many men, men the Boxed T could ill spare.

While the dun sucked thirstily as it stood hock-deep in the wide, sandy ford, Bill's eyes sought the most tempting shade. He headed the pony toward willows, pushed through into the deepest shade and stepped out of the saddle.

For a while, he lay outstretched, every muscle relaxed, gratefully soaking in the silence and solitude. He dozed, while the dun muzzled the clumped grass and flicked idly at the flies.

Of a sudden Bill snapped awake and sat up. Something was amiss. He glanced quickly around. The dun had ceased cropping. Its head was up and ears erect, pointing across the river. He jumped up and scanned the simmering plain through the screen of chaparral. Two riders were approaching at an easy lope from the east, their faces shaded by the flopping brims of black sombreros. The sun glinted upon brass buttons and plated spurs. Vaqueros, on Boxed T range!

Cautiously, Bill led his pony deeper into the brush. knotted its reins around a smooth willow and crept back to the water's edge. The strangers were close now. Bill recognized the breed, akin to the three who had jumped him in Painted Rock. Laughing and jabbering, they dropped down to the ford, splashed across the stream and swung to the ground on the further side.

A gnarled old cottonwood stood alone beside the trail, stained by flood and scarred by storm. One rider held a square of white against the trunk, while the other tacked it in place with a chunk of rock.

Curiosity moved the peering Bill. This had to be looked into—pronto. Bent low, he injuned toward the two riders. Their backs were toward him and they were intent upon their job. Moving fast, Bill slid through the patched brush, was not a dozen paces distant when the jingle of his spur chains brought the pair around in startled surprise.

"*Buenos dias,* señors!" greeted Bill genially. "How come yore ridin' Box T range?"

Two pairs of belligerent dark eyes measured him from swarthy poker faces. The right hand of one twitched toward his knife hilt, but checked at a hissed warning from his companion.

Bill stepped closer, eyed the white sheet above their shoulders. The message it carried was brief and to the point:

TAKE WARNING!

To the Boxed T—the river is your boundary. Cross at your peril.

Pancho Hernandez.

"So thet's the play!" There was a smile upon Bill's lips but none in his eyes. "Say—you!" He nodded at the Mexican who had betrayed an itch to use his knife. "Yank thet sheet down, careful. I got a use f'r it."

The vaquero hesitated, feet shuffling uneasily, scowling at the youthful gringo.

"Rattle your hocks!" snapped Bill.

Like unleased steel springs, Pancho's two henchmen galvanized into action. In a blur of motion, one snapped at his sheathed knife, the other stabbed for his gun. But Bill's .44's were up and out, bucking and stabbing crimson fire. Blood ran like red wine from four ears, each neatly perforated in the fleshy lobe. Guns and knives were forgotten as the pair yelped in agony and clapped their hands against their bloody heads.

"Yank thet sheet down!" barked Bill, smoking guns held hip-high.

One swung around and hastily pulled the notice off the trunk with sticky red fingers.

"Tear it in half—careful!" directed their tormentor, inexorably. "Now eat it—half each!"

Protest poured in liquid Spanish from the bleeding vaqueros' thick lips. Bill's gun barrels came up grimly. "It's high and center next time," he promised, with stark emphasis. "Get thet chow down yore gizzards!"

Desperately, the scared vaqueros stuffed the ragged strips of paper into their mouths. Watchfully, Bill stood guard while jaws champed feverishly. Finally, the unpalatable meal was disposed of.

"Now light a shuck!" ordered Bill. "And show yore boss them neat earmarks. Tell Pancho the first time I ketch him on Boxed T range I aim tuh decorate his ears likewise, with fancy upper crops. *Adios!*"

The two gory P H riders jumped for their ponies and hit the ford in a cascade of spray, eager to put distance between themselves and this deadly, fast-shooting stranger.

Bill watched until rising dust plumes veiled the fleeing men, then headed for his pony.

As he approached Painted Rock, huddled beneath the frowning bastions of the great butte, a score of windows threw back reflections of the setting sun like flashing heliographs.

Main Street was quiet, too quiet, ruminated Bill, as his pony stirred the dust between rows of empty hitch rails. Seemed like there wasn't a puncher in town, except around The Highway to Hell, where a handful of disconsolate riders, the former Boxed T waddies, hunkered beneath the wooden canopy and eyed him stonily when he reined up to the rail and peeled out of leather.

Through the dusty saloon windows, Bill sighted more riders inside, sprawled listlessly around the tables. Pete Lastro's big form bulked at the bar, in earnest confab with the redheaded town marshal.

Eleven good gunhands, considered Bill regretfully, gone to waste. By sundown on the morrow, other outfits in the Valley would have grabbed them and they'd be throwing lead against instead of for the Boxed T. All old-timers, too, the backbone of Thompson's crew. And he could read from the weariness in their eyes and the sag in their shoulders that they wished they were back in the Boxed T bunkhouse. He knew, too, that these weather-beaten waddies were too stiff-necked to admit it. Gosh, how he needed those guns! And dammit, he swore softly, savagely, he'd get them back.

He stepped up to the bar amid bleak silence. Lastro's mouth snapped shut like a steel trap and the redheaded marshal slewed around.

"Howdy boss!" he greeted dryly. "Yuh shore stepped into Jim's boots quick—and onto Pete's toes!"

Bill shrugged and poured a short drink. "Pete's too all-fired techy," he flung back offhandedly. "Jim Thompson said tuh ride in and brace him, but I see he's in a sod-pawin', horn-tossin' mood."

"Quit yore pantin' and gimme Jim's message," growled the foreman.

"I reckon the boys would want in on this," demurred Bill.

"Hey, fellers!" roared Lastro. "This leather-slapper brought word from Jim."

Boots pounded on the plankwalk and chairs scraped hastily as the ex-Boxed T waddies suddenly came to violent life. In seconds, they packed around the group at the bar, inquiring eyes on the self-appointed messenger.

"Boys," began Bill gravely, "looks like Jim Thompson's due tuh strum a harp. And he's mighty low in spirits. He figgered you hairpins would stick tighter than a mustard plaster when he got in a tight—and yuh done rode out on him!" He waited until the rumble of protest subsided. "I know why yuh quit—yuh jest didn't cotton tuh me, but what yuh don't know is this—the Boxed T's got twenty-three hands, tuh buck five outfits musterin' seventy or more, and thet's not figgerin' nesters. Wal, I put up a deal tuh Thompson—make me ramrod of the Boxed T and I'll bring in twenty more fighting men, old pards. Thet'll give us more than forty guns—plenty tuh whip hell outta the lobos skulkin' around Boxed T range. Jim was in a jack pot and I handed him a pat hand. He grabbed it. Wouldn't you? Wal, his word is thus—yuh get back tuh where yuh belong and I'll drift in later with plenty more guns. Jim feels bad about you jaspers and sight of yore maps u'll do him more good than all the sawbones in Arizona."

Bill paused—his words had run out. He was no speechmaker.

Silence followed his appeal. Men fidgeted uncertainly and eyes sought the foreman for guidance.

Town Marshal Jack Goodmer was the first to speak. "Ef you boys don't hightail f'r the spread, I'm damned ef I won't jug yuh f'r a bunch of lousy sheepherders!" His voice was easy, friendly, but it held a stinging note of contempt.

"I ain't takin' orders from no gun-totin' colt," barked Lastro.

"Yuh don't have to get riled over me," put in Bill mildly. "I'm driftin' jest as soon as the shootin's over. I'm no cowman."

"Aw, heck, Pete!" burst out a graying puncher. "Le's git back tuh the spread!"

"The word's got around thet yore yeller quitters, ridin' out of gunsmoke," threw in the marshal carelessly.

"Yeller!" roared an old-timer. "I reckon we gotta show 'em. Le's go, boys!"

With joyous whoops, the punchers stampeded for the batwings. Pete Lastro clumped heavily after them. Dust billowed outside as excited men untied their ponies and whirled southward.

Wild yippees died in the distance. Bill and the redheaded marshal were left alone in the saloon.

"Thanks, pard!" said Bill fervently, with a deep-drawn breath. "Ef yuh hadn't thrown in, I'd have been stuck."

"Hell's bells!" grinned the rangy Goodmer, "them mavericks was jest itchin tuh get back. They been ridin' f'r Jim so long the Boxed T is home. And whar's this big bunch—twenty men, it seems yuh said—acomin' from?"

"What other bunch?" inquired Bill, innocently.

"Yore old pards."

"Goshawmighty!" grinned Bill, "I clean forgot them. I reckon, mebbe, they done strayed."

"You gosh-durned hogswiggler!" chuckled the marshal. "There ain't ten good men loose in the whole Valley. Wal, you'll need 'em, pard!"

Bill youred himself another drink. His brief surge of triumph receded. Although he'd succeeded in roping the dozen runaways, the Boxed T was still outnumbered two to one. "Yuh got any ideas?" he asked hopefully.

Goodmer shook his head. "Everyone's done took sides, and the shooting's due tuh start. Yuh can't buy any more chips in this game. Wal, reckon I'll beat it f'r home, the town's quieter than boothill."

Bill nursed his bourbon along and mulled over the manpower problem.

Like a string of firecrackers exploding, rifle shot punched through the quiet of gathering night. His drink forgotten, Bill hastily hit for the street, the barkeep pushing on his heels. They stood in the gloom outside, listening. Up and down street, doors were opening and heads dabbed out. The town marshal came back along the plankwalk at a half run.

Heavier now, the lash of gunfire cut through the night, the vicious spanging of Winchesters mingling with the deeper boom of forty-fives.

"What's the trouble?" yelled Bill, as Goodmer came abreast.

"You tell me!" snapped the marshal. "Sounds like it's south of the river. I gamble yore boys rode into trouble, but who in hell would make trouble right in our back yard?"

He loosed a pony tied near by and swung into leather. Bill jumped across the plankwalk and untied the dun. Together, they rode downstreet, toward the sound of crackling gunfire.

On the outskirts of town, a pony's hooves played a mad tattoo on the heat-hardened stage road ahead. The animal streaked past in the gloom, neck outstretched, tail streaming. Bill caught a glimpse of a bald-headed man sagging across its withers, grabbing leather with both hands.

"Thet's Baldy!" yelled Goodmer and whirled his mount. Bill brought the dun around. Dust and pebbles flew as they spurred in pursuit of the hurtling Boxed T rider.

When they hit Main Street at full gallop, townsmen were running toward the shack that served as marshal's office. Dim in the fading light, Baldy was stretched out on the plankwalk. Two men knelt beside him, ripping away his gray shirt with clasp knives—it was wet with blood. A rapidly growing throng circled the wounded man, amid a mumble of excited talk.

The marshal elbowed a path through the crowd, Bill behind him. They leaned over the recumbent rider.

"How come yuh got hit, Baldy?" asked Goodmer.

The veteran Boxed T hand looked up with pain-weary eyes. "Et's thet bustard Pancho and his vaqueros. Bunch of 'em jumped us by the ford. The rattlesnakes was holed up both sides of the trail. Pete and four other fellers was ridin' ahead. They tumbled fust crack outta the box. I was tailin' the bunch. Gamble there warn't a man rode clear 'cept me."

Cold dismay chilled Bill. The powder barrel had exploded at last, when he least expected it. And the blast had blown away a third of the Boxed T crew.

CHAPTER NINE

"PANCHO'S A DEVIL, when he's aroused," said the marshal, lowvoiced to Bill. "I'll lay odds somethin' set him on the rampage." The chunky rider thought of the earmarked vaqueros and remained glumly silent. Goodmer threw open the door of the office, removed the glass chimney from a bracketed lamp and set a match to the wick. His roped blanket roll was propped in a corner. He spread the soogans on the floor and two townsmen packed in Baldy's limp form.

Doc Blaine's plump figure wedged through the throng. He bobbed briskly through the doorway and gave the bloodied Baldy a quick glance. Dumping his black bag on the floor, he slipped off his coat, folded it and laid it on the seat of a chair.

"Say, Doc!" drawled the marshal. "Seems like there's plenty more work f'r yuh down by the ford."

"This would occur just when I'm clean out of coffins!" There was a touch of asperity in the doctor's voice. "Should have kept my stock up, with this infernal range war brewing." He rolled up his sleeves and opened his bag.

Goodmer shooed out curious stragglers and firmly closed the door. The doctor sank down on his knees beside the wounded man.

Thirty minutes later, a sober cavalcade followed the curves of the wagon road south. The marshal and Bill jogged ahead. Behind them, trailed Doc Blaine and six apprehensive townsmen, each leading a spare pony.

A mile from town the forlorn cottonwoods that lined the river bank thrust up into the night like ragged specters. Wan stars peered down at the silence-shrouded mesquite flats and the night breeze rustled eerily through the dry grass.

Movement by the river brought a smothered exclamation from a jittery townsman. Warily, the string of riders pulled down to a walk, stiff in their saddles; relaxed when the outlines of several riderless ponies, aimlessly drifting through the brush, became plain. Tension gripped them again when they saw gray-shirted bodies lumped on the wagon road before them, twisted and contorted in death. In taut silence, the marshal and Bill stepped down and moved from one form to another, while the townsmen sat their ponies, uneasy eyes searching the shadows.

"Guess we won't need yuh, Doc," reported the marshal dryly. "Pancho's boys rubbed out every last man."

"Murdered 'em!" cut in Bill. "Yuh ain't tellin' me they was killed clean. Them bushwacking rattlesnakes beefed 'em after they was down."

"Wal, they're daid!" Even the dare-devil marshal's voice was subdued in face of the wholesale killing. He laid a kindly hand upon Bill's shoulder, "What's done can't be undone. Pack 'em on the ponies, boys!"

"Nine cadavers," lamented the plump doctor, "and not a coffin nearer than Deever."

"Ten," corrected Bill somberly.

"Doc's right," supplied Goodmer, "Pete don't seem tuh be around."

"But Baldy claimed he was ridin' ahead, with four other fellers, and dropped first crack outta the box."

"Ef Baldy was tailin' the bunch, he didn't see much, in thet light," pointed out the marshal. "But mebbe we missed Pete. Le's take another looksee."

Together, they searched the dim-lit wagon road, from the bunched townsmen to the ford, but there was no sign of the foreman's body.

"Queer!" mused Goodmer.

The dreary procession wound back to town and to the barn which served as mortuary.

Bill tied his pony again outside The Highway to Hell, glanced over the batwings at the yammering patrons packed three-deep at the bar and turned away. He was in no mood for talk—there were nine dead men on his mind.

A lamp still burned above the counter of Tess Goodmer's eating house. As he pushed through the fly curtains, the coppery-haired girl broke away from a chittering group of women and hurried in behind him. He jammed his hat upon a peg and slid on a stool.

"Howdy, boss!" greeted Tess pertly, rounding the counter.

He nodded glumly.

With a quick glance at his set features, she moved into the kitchen, emerged with a steaming coffee pot. Without further word, she set a mug before him and poured.

Absently, he added sugar and sipped slowly.

"Well, at least you might thank me for serving you after hours," she commented.

He grunted, still lost in abstraction.

"It hit you hard, didn't it?" she said quietly.

"I figgered on fightin' men, not rattlesnakes."

"What did you expect Pancho to do—serve written notice?"

"B'gawd, yore sidin' the skunk!" he exploded.

"Pancho is in this fight to win, he has his own code and he's certainly not yellow," she came back defensively. Tess did not add that the graceful Mexican had once quirted a calloused muleskinner on Main Street for mouthing an off-color remark as she passed.

"Wal, ef thet don't beat all creation, yuh sidin' with Pancho!" Coffee slopped on the varnished counter as Bill banged his mug down. Her gray eyes met his accusing glare in subtle challenge. Plainly disgusted, he grabbed his Stetson and pushed out into the street. Deep in his own dejection, he elbowed past knots of townsmen who still lingered on the darkened plankwalks. Tess Goodmer siding that yellow bushwhacker! It was the last straw. Why he was so much interested in the pert young woman's ideas he probably could not have explained. But her seeming defection stirred him almost as much as the killings. He reached The Highway to Hell, stood outside uncertainly. "Doggone it!" he muttered, "I feel lower than a snake's belly."

Immersed in gloom, he untied the dun and headed out of town. There was but one place to go—the ranch. And instead of leading back a bunch of men as he had boasted, he'd bring nothing but calamity. One-third of the Boxed T crew wiped out before he was set to fight. He sure had proved one heck of a boss.

Night lay heavy on the range when he reached the river crossing where he had earmarked Pancho's two vaqueros earlier in the day. The water gurgled, dark and sullen, around his pony's hocks as it splashed across the ford. Dimly, the old cottonwood loomed ahead—and there was a square white patch upon its gnarled trunk.

Bill stepped down, struck a match and read the lettering. Pancho had posted another warning. The gall of the greaser! With an angry growl, Bill dropped the match and ripped the sheet down. At the same moment a loop snaked silently from the obscurity of the branches above and dropped on his shoulders. Before the surprised rider could duck or throw it off, his hidden assailant jerked hard. The pliant rawhide slid swiftly through the honda, tightened around Bill's neck, bit deep into the flesh. Choking, he stabbed for his guns. They roared and bucked in stuttering thunder as he emptied them into the branches overhead. Remorselessly, the noose bit deeper. Limbs jerking in the throes of strangulation, he was hauled off his feet. His guns thudded to the ground as he tore frenziedly at the slender rope that was throttling him. Thunder filled his ears and he floated away into deep, velvet depths.

The searing pain of a red-hot ring around his neck shocked him back to consciousness. Pistons pounding in his head, he swayed to his feet. Again the ring contracted, and he fought for air. Pancho's voice, smooth as slow-flowing oil, registered in his ears. "Do not touch the so beautiful necklace, Señor Carson, or we sweeng you again." The loop slackened, and the prisoner sucked in great lungfuls of air.

Dimly, he discerned the forms of three black-sombreroed Mexicans; two had bloodstained bandanas wrapped around their heads. Pancho's mocking tones continued to flow into his ears, "You are so simple, señor. You theenk you can make horseplay weeth Pancho Hernandez. First you weeng two of my vaqueros, then you shoot holes in the ears of Sancho and José. We are just greasers, spics, chili-eaters, eh?" His voice steeled with bitter irony. "We are like the jackass, to be keeked and mocked and shot. I, Pancho am no jackass. You weel hang!"

Bill stood silent. He was thrown and hog-tied. At the first sign of resistance, a flip of the *reata* would choke the life out of him.

"But, before you hang," continued Pancho silkily, "you weel eat." Smooth features mantled in a genial smile, he held out the notice Bill had ripped off the tree trunk.

The palms of the prisoner's damp hands fondled his empty holsters. Still dizzy with vertigo, he faced the P/H boss with locked lips.

Pancho sighed, motioned to the vaquero who held the drooping rope's end. Reaching high, the rider threw his weight on the rope. Again Bill was hauled off the ground—choking, kicking and struggling—again he lapsed into merciful oblivion.

The painful impact of sharp-toed boots against his ribs brought him back to gasping life. He staggered to his feet and again faced the still-smiling Pancho. "You eat?" inquired the latter solicitously.

Numbly Bill nodded, attempted to reach for the crumpled sheet. His arm dropped weakly. The Mexican stepped closer, hand outstretched. Senses still reeling, Bill measured the distance, grabbed Pancho's wrist with his right hand and jerked. Taken by surprise, the P/H boss lurched forward. With the strength of desperation, the prisoner's left hand fastened upon his throat, and his right latched beside it. Girded by grim fury, his fingers sank into the yielding flesh. Now the greaser would know how it felt to choke!

Pancho writhed and fought, clawing madly for his prisoner's eyes. Bill wrapped his legs around the madly twisting Mexican, cradled his face against the other's chest, fending off Pancho's tearing fingers with his elbows. In silent ferocity they swayed, intertwined. With a fierce surge of triumph, Bill felt the Mexican's muscles relax. The writhing became feebler. Then the startled vaqueros came to life, leapt for the slack rope's end. Too late! Bill snatched a pearl-handled gun from the holster of the feebly writhing, half-insensible Pancho. Orange fire stabbed the darkness and the two vaqueros—one stumbling—stampeded blindly for their ponies. Water cascaded as the animals hit the ford at full gallop. Then there was silence, save for the hoarse wheezing of Pancho, writhing spasmodically upon the ground, and the fast dying thud of racing hooves.

His neck ringed with fire, Bill jerked at the loose-hanging *reata* and the slack rawhide hissed softly over the branch above. Leaning against the tree trunk for support, he gingerly loosened the noose. Numbing pain shot through his head at every movement. Pancho's slow-twisting form was as silent as a shadow. The Mexican had ceased to wheeze. Quiet as a copperhead, considered Bill—and as dangerous.

"Thou shalt not steal, saith the Lord!" Deep and forceful, a voice boomed from the night.

Flicking Pancho's gun from beneath his waistband, Bill slewed around, eyes searching the darkness.

The form of a man bulked before him. In the gloom the stranger seemed as big as a bear. Again a mighty voice boomed,

"But verily the Lord is good—to a measly rustler! For a while I thought that, in his wisdom, he was minded to allow them greasers to stretch your neck. But he is ever-merciful. Repent, my son, repent!" His voice dropped and he added matter-of-factly, "I never had much use for greasers, anyways."

"Rustlers!" choked Bill angrily. "Where in hell did yuh get thet notion? Pancho and his blasted bushwhackers done blasted a dozen men tonight. They jumped me at the ford."

"Speak further, brother," requested the burly stranger, looming above Bill. "I am from afar, carrying the message of salvation into the wilderness."

Bill steadied against the tree, fighting a quaver in his knees. "Thet Pancho," he began. "who's twistin' like a doggoned rattler right behind yuh—" The stranger turned, searching. His head came around again in swift interrogation, "I see no body."

With a growl, Bill lurched forward, staggering past his strange vistor—Pancho had vanished. Then a spasm of retching gripped Bill, his senses whirled and darkness enveloped him.

A beard brushed his cheek as he was lifted and thrown across a broad shoulder as though he were a sack of grain. With long, easy strides the big man headed downstream, brushed through hedged chaparral and pushed deep into a willow thicket. There he dumped his load beside the glowing embers of a small campfire, on the edge of which a sooted coffee pot was set. He spilled coffee into a tin cup, lifted Bill's drooping head and trickled the warm liquid between his lips. This done, he tossed an armful of dry twigs into the fire, hunkered down beside it and casually built a smoke.

After awhile, the twice-hanged rider struggled to a sitting position, fondling his gouged throat. He blinked stupidly around, striving to think coherently. Plain in the fitful light of the flickering flames, the bearded stranger regarded him with piercing eyes, set like twin pieces of glass in the dark mahogany of his features. He was a burly, rawboned fellow, with unkempt bushy beard and a mane of jet-black hair that curled down to his shoulders. Wide open, a cheap cotton shirt exposed a thatch of hair upon his barrel chest. A strip of rawhide secured his trail-grimed pants above the hips, and the bottoms were thrust into high boots. Around the waist sagged a gunbelt. Over all was draped an ill-fitting rusty frock coat, the tails of which sagged in the dust.

"Thanks, mister!" Bill's voice was a strained whisper. He gratefully sipped more coffee to ease his aching throat, then told of the Grass Valley feud and his part in it.

"Surely the Lord guided the footsteps of his servant aright," boomed the stranger, when he concluded. "This is indeed a fruitful pasture."

"Say, what are you mister," croaked Bill curiously, "Prospector or gambler?"

"Brother, I am Paul the Preacher, a humble servant of the Lord, who hath inspired me to save souls in this ungodly valley."

Bill's eyes strayed to the shaggy evangelist's gun. "Yore well-heeled—f'r a preacher."

Paul's firm lips twitched, "Brother, I am armed with righteousness, but a six gun packs a potent argument." His keen eyes dwelt upon Bill. "So you rod the Boxed T—outnumbered and surrounded by the hosts of the wicked?"

"And not a gun to be hired in the whole danged valley."

The preacher thoughtfully stroked his beard, eying the fire. "There are men aplenty," he boomed finally. "Evil men, it is true, but fast on the draw, and not more than a long day's ride away from here."

"Where?" demanded Bill eagerly.

"They are men with a price upon their heads, brother. Outlaws, harder to handle than unbroken colts."

"I kin handle 'em."

Paul smiled grimly. "Three greasers handled you, brother. I fear you are puffed with the pride of youth. Pride goeth before destruction and a haughty spirit before a fall."

Bill rose cautiously to his feet, caressed his rope-galled throat, pushed unsteadily through the brush toward the river bank. The cool water felt like balm. Surer-footed now, he headed back to the cottonwood, groped around until he found his guns, cleaned and reloaded them, tossed Pancho's gun aside. Easier in mind, he located the dun by the water's edge, heaved painfully into the saddle and returned to the strange evangelist's camp.

Across the fire, he again eyed the bearded Paul. Something in his cold stare brought the preacher to his feet.

"Go f'r yore gun!" ordered Bill bleakly.

For a split second, the evangelist hesitated, then his right hand whipped down. He was no slouch on the draw, conceded Bill, but before the long-barreled Colt cleared leather, he blinked into twin barrels, leveled upon his middle. His grip relaxed and the Colt slid down into the holster again.

"You are fast, brother," he boomed, "I have never met faster—is this the way you repay a good Samaritan?"

Bill's tight features relaxed in a quick grin. "Nope, Preacher—d'yuh still figger I can't handle them outlaws?"

Paul carressed his beard, "Maybe you can, brother—maybe!"

The younger man replaced his guns. "Wal, le's get down tuh cases—I can use them hombres. Where are they?"

The bearded man stirred up the fire with his boot, again hunkered beside it. He made no reply, but dove into a tail pocket of his shabby frock coat and yanked out a folded wad of paper. Carefully, he smoothed the dog-eared sheet. Watching curiously, bill recognized the black print of a frayed reward notice. Before the preacher extended it, he had a swift hunch as to the identity of the wanted man—and his hunch hit the bull's-eye. The black capitals jumped up at him:

$5,000 REWARD
Wanted for Murder
Jules Lefevre, alias Lightning Lefevre …

He didn't need to read further.

Paul's voice rumbled in his ears, "Would you know the whereabouts of that sinner, brother?"

"How in heck would I know the jasper?" came back Bill impatiently. "This notice is twenty-five years old, ef it's a day. Hell, I warn't around them days."

"You pack his guns, brother," returned Paul imperturbably.

"Yore loco!"

"The stocks are branded, brother," advised the preacher softly.

Then Bill remembered. Burnt into each butt, protruding from its open-top holster, were the initials "L.L." And it flashed upon him that if this psalm-singing hombre noticed them, so probably had Fiddlefoot. But how come this fellow was so plumb anxious to meet up with his paw?

CHAPTER TEN

BILL'S EYES NARROWED as he met the preacher's accusing stare.

"I won these guns in a poker game, 'way back in Texas." He flung the lie with cool challenge.

"How long since, brother?"

Bill shrugged. "So long I ferget. Now how about them outlaws, mister, not more'n a long day's ride?"

"Brother," came back Paul dryly, "I plumb forgot just where they are."

For a full minute the eyes of the pair locked in silent conflict. Bill was the first to give ground. "How come yore so mighty curious about—Lightning Lefevre?"

"There is an accounting, brother, long overdue."

"Lightning is my paw."

"I guessed as much, brother." Paul's voice was without malice. "You use his draw and, to give the devil his due, he schooled you well."

"He ain't in no shape f'r gunfightin' these days—both his legs been paralyzed f'r years."

"Just penance for his misdeeds, brother."

"Quit dribblin', mister!" Bill's voice was brittle. "Yore talkin' of my paw."

But Paul ignored him, staring moodily into the flames. "The Good Book counsels, return good for evil," he muttered. Then he roused and again gave attention to the young rider. "Your pardon, brother, I was wrastling with the devil. Go, sleep in peace.

At sunup I shall reveal where you may gather the spawn of Satan, men with guns, but without souls. But when you return, armored gainst your enemies, what is your plan of action?"

Bill's forehead furrowed. "Reckon I'll jest—fight."

Paul smiled with tolerant amusement. "Even though you bring back a score of gunmen, your enemies will still be as the locust. Would you waste your scanty strength in blind battle? In unity there is strength. United, brother, your enemies will prevail. Separate them and you will shatter them."

"Say, I guess yuh got something there," admitted Bill slowly.

The preacher chuckled. "Wise counsel, brother, from the Good Book. And where were you raised in Texas?"

So smoothly was the question added, that San Andreas was on the tip of Bill's tongue before he realized its significance. With a quick glance at Paul's bland features, he retorted, "North of the Rio Grande."

"A right broad stretch of country," murmured the other, unabashed. He rose, wrapped his voluminous frock coat around his burly form and stretched out, feet to the fire. "*Buenas noches,* brother—and pleasant dreams."

For a while, Bill hunkered by the dying coals, pondering on the events of the day, and then he sank into the deep sleep of exhaustion.

Pulsating beneath the fierce rays of the sun, the desert lapped away into hazy infinity. A tiny dust streamer crawled across its barren breast, rising from the hooves of a jaded dun, grayed, like its rider, by the choking dust fog that floated around them like a pall. For an eternity, it seemed to Bill, he had beaten southward across the endless waste. The sun was dropping westward and he had shared the last few mouthfuls of water in his canteen with the dun an hour before. But still his eyes, aching from sun glare, could glimpse no sign of the red butte that the preacher said lay due north of El Infierno.

He caught a dull-red gleam across the cactus-scabbed barrens ahead. Hope stirred anew. Squinting eagerly from beneath the down-turned brim of his Stetson, he saw that the rays of the setting sun were gleaming upon the lofty side of a great red butte. When the dun labored through yielding sand past the ruddy pile, shadows were fast marching across the desert.

Upon the flats, not a mile distant, were a handful of yellowed adobes, bunched around a boxlike structure. Beyond the sun-scorched dreariness of these human habitations a patch of chaparral showed soothing green, which meant water, and therefore life, to the renegades who lurked in El Infierno.

Through bunched bear grass and skeleton ocatillos, the weary rider wound toward the outlaw settlement, set in the heart of the barrens, a bare mile below the Border.

Slatternly women eyed him dully as he rode past squat adobes. Hogs, goats and naked children rooted indiscriminately in the dust, thick-littered with discarded tin cans and empty bottles. Ragged mestizos dozed in the lengthening shadows. A cur snapped at the dun's heels.

He reined up before the square, frame building. It was two stories high, unpainted and weather-beaten. A row of small windows gaped on the second floor, uncurtained, cracked and broken. A drunken vauqero sagged against a water barrel, staring stupidly.

Across the front of the building a rotting wooden canopy gave scant shade. Dirty fly curtains draped a wide doorway, faintly illumined by the sickly yellow light of an oil lamp that burned within. If a more desolate dump existed, thought Bill, in disgust, he had never come across it. But saddled ponies were tied thick at the hitch rail and the deep rumble of many voices reached his ears. The preacher had spoken truly—here were guns.

He peeled out of leather, tied the footsore pony, crossed to the barrel and shouldered the reeling Mexican out of the way. He dipped his Stetson into the barrel and carried it back to the dun, the crown filled with water. The pony snorted dust and sucked thirstily. Then Bill swept the curtains aside and stepped into what he judged was a cantina.

Not a head turned as he stood by the doorway, his eyes slowly adjusting to the subdued light. Facing him, a rough plank bar ran across the rear of the room. At one side, an uncarpeted stairway led to the second floor. Spurred riders and wide-sombreroed vaqueros idled at the bar, served by a thick-set Mexican, hog fat, whose triple chins wobbled with every movement. Small tables were strewn across the beaten-earth floor, around which hard-faced hombres were hunched. Pungent oaths punctuated the soft slap of cards and jingle of coin.

Bill threaded through the tables and stepped up to the bar beside a hatchet-faced gunman, with stubbled jaw and a pair of walnut-butted forty-fived thonged over corduroy pants.

The barkeep waddled up, chins aquiver. "Shot of bourbon!" ordered Bill. The gunman turned and weighed him impersonally, brooding eyes alive with eternal watchfulness.

"Howdy!" greeted Bill. "I'm spittin' cinders."

The other nodded curtly, thin, saturnine features impressionless. Sparse gray hair straggled from beneath his rolled-brim Stetson, and life had set its mark in the deep-etched lines around his thin lips. A red feather, thrust through his hatband, supplied the one vivid touch of color against his gray garb. Dangerous as dynamite, decided Bill.

He trickled more bourbon into his glass and loosened his bandana.

The gunman's tight lips quirked at sight of the red weal around his neck. "Rope branded, eh?" he drawled, and his voice was as soft as a woman's.

"Yuh said it!" grinned Bill. "And it sure cured me of necktie parties."

"They call me Red," volunteered the other.

"Glad t'meet yuh! I'm Bill Carson from Painted Rock. I come tuh hire guns."

"Yeah?" The gunman's bleak eyes were as expressionless as his voice.

"Range war!" amplified Bill.

Red scarcely raised his voice, yet it cut through the buzz of talk around them. "Hey, git a load of this, yuh gun-totin' lobos, ef yuh crave action. This hairpin's hirin' guns."

From the quick silence that draped the cantina, Bill guessed that the man beside him packed plenty weight. He turned, faced a battery of hard, unblinking eyes. He cleared his throat.

"Wal, I'll cut it short, boys. I rod the Boxed T, fifty miles or so north. We got trouble with other outfits and we need guns. Pay's a hundred a month, and plenty good chuck."

"Ef yuh rod it, I gamble it's a two-bit spread," sneered a bitterfaced hombre, wire-thin, seated at a near-by table.

"Hold yore hawses, Gleeko!" purred Red. "Me, I kinda took a shine tuh this cockerel. The Boxed T's the biggest spread in Grass Valley."

"Old man Thompson rods it," threw in another.

"Thet proves the hombre's runnin' a sandy," rasped Gleeko. "He's as crazy as popcorn on a hot stove."

"I done took over," said Bill shortly, "and here's dinero tuh back my talk." He stepped toward the card table, around which the man called Gleeko and three others were sprawled, yanked a leather pouch from his pants pocket and spilled a stream of yellow double eagles between two half-empty whisky bottles. It was Crawler's gold, from the chest in Panther Gulch.

The bitter-faced desperado spat deliberately on Bill's boot. "Me, I'm not stringin' along with no feudin' cowman who don't know sick 'em, but let thet dinero lay. I kin use it."

Hoarse laughter flooded into Bill's ears. A rheumy-eyed rider, sitting opposite his tormentor, grabbed greedily for the pile of gold. He yelped and snatched back his hand as Bill's gun barrel cracked his knuckles. Gleeko mouthed an oath, reached forward with his left hand and grabbed a gun butt with the right. In a split second Bill's guns roared and lanced lead. The two bottles tinkled into fragments. Black gunsmoke swirled heavily as broken glass and whisky sprayed over the seated men. Chairs crashed as they flung backward, arms thrown up instinctively to protect their faces. Eyes venomous, the bitter-faced gunman gathered himself off the floor, blood dripping from his chin.

Bill dropped his smoking sixes back into leather, spread his arms. "Wal, mister," he taunted, "le's see ef yuh can beat a cowman, who don't know sick 'em, to the draw."

In an instant the confusion was stilled. Men shuffled quickly away from the pair. Greeko's right hand inched for his gun. Red's soft voice broke into an expectant quiet, "Guess the jasper's got what it takes. Me, I'm f'r him. Who craves tuh git potbellied, sittin' around swillin' rotgut? Any lawman around Painted Rock, feller?"

"Nope!" came back Bill promptly, gaze still glued upon the scowling Gleeko. "Sheriff's settin' out this hand. County seat's forty miles away."

"Wal, we gotta chew it over. And lay off, Gleeko!" His purr reminded Bill of a panther—with unsheathed claws. The bitter-faced man shuffled back, growling beneath his breath. Bill gathered up his gold, pooled in the spilt whisky.

"Whar did yuh pick them guns up, kid?" He jumped at Red's sibilant whisper. Silently, the gunman had cat-toed up beside him.

"What's it tuh yuh?" he flung back.

"Plenty!" There was deadly emphasis in the tersely spoken word, emphasis that whirled Bill around braced for action. Red's pale eyes held the young rider's, "A double-crossin' bustard—Lightnin' Lefevre—packed them guns, oncet."

CHAPTER ELEVEN

SILENTLY, BUT NO LESS FERVENTLY, Bill cursed the telltale initials burnt on the butts of Crawler's guns—they stirred trouble wherever he went. "Red," he returned patiently, "mebbe this Lefevre hairpin packed these irons once, but I own 'em now. Wouldn't yuh reckon Lefevre's planted, long since?"

"Yep," admitted the gunman, "guess I got choused up over nothing. Renegades packed thick around the purring gunman. The rising sun silvered the cholla and glinted upon the metal of a hard-bitten bunch riding north from El Infierno. At their head rode Bill, sternly repressing an urge to give vent to his exhilaration by exuberant yippees. Beside him, Red sat loose in the saddle, brooding eyes devouring distance. Behind them jingled eighteen men.

The Boxed T rider breathed deep of the tangy desert air. His thoughts leapt ahead, framing a plan of action. He pulled Mildred Thompson's rough map out of his vest pocket, opened it up and scrutinized the layout of the Valley. Two ranches lay between the Boxed T and the Border, separated from their neighbors by Thompson's vast expanse of range—the Lazy H and the Frying Pan. Chris Hansen of the Lazy H had ten hands on his pay roll, while the Limey who ran the Frying Pan tallied six. If he could cut them both out of the ruckus with a swift stroke, the odds would even up. Neither would be expecting an attack from the south. He had the advantage of surprise and a force of nineteen seasoned gunfighters. The job should be easy.

"Say, Red!" He broke into the saturnine gunman's brooding introspection. "Take a gander at this map!" The other silently held out a gloved hand. Eagerly, Bill outlined his plan. Red listened with unmoved features. "Hunky-dory!" he approved. "We should ketch 'em with their pants down."

It was sundown before they reached the edge of the grasslands and sighted Lazy H beef. Bill headed for Rocky Spring, the nearest water, located on Lazy H range. Ponies and riders were jaded after the grueling grind across the desert. He planned to rest his force overnight at the spring and hit Hansen's spread at dawn. There was a chance that a range rider might sight the bunch of strange horsemen and spread the alarm, but that chance had to be taken.

Rocky Spring lay in low rolling hills about five miles west of the ranch house, according to the map. With gathering darkness, its exact location troubled Bill until he noticed the long lines of cows threaded across the flats, drifting northwest—and followed them. Before night fell they rode into a cut where water seeped from crevices in the rocky hillside and dribbled into a muddied pool, fringed with chaparral.

Hock-deep in the pool, cows scattered in panic as the dust-smothered renegades gave the ponies their heads and thundered down to the spring. Bill flashed a saddled pony in the brush. A solitary puncher rose hastily from where he had been hunkered beside the pool and dashed for his mount. Before he had taken three clumsy steps in his high-heeled riding boots, the advancing horsemen enveloped him. A shot split the low thunder of drumming hooves. The running man pitched forward, shot in the back, and the galloping riders swept over his body.

Gleeko dropped his six gun back into leather. The dead rider forgotten, saddle-weary, thirsty men piled out of their saddles at the pool. Anger in his blue eyes, Bill pushed through the press toward the bitter-faced bandit. Nothing stirred him more than wanton killing.

"Say, did yuh have tuh down thet jasper?" he demanded.

Gleeko's lips twisted with faint amusement, "Ain't we hired tuh fight?"

"Yuh call thet fightin', pluggin' the poor devil in the back?"

"One less tuh kill, ain't there?" retorted Gleeko, with a thin laugh.

"It ain't my way."

"Wal, it's mine. Now chew on thet—boss!" And the bitter-faced bandit turned contemptuously away.

Fuming, Bill stood irresolute, conscious of the amused glances that the hard cases around were throwing at him. And he realized the significance of the preacher's cryptic "Maybe" when he so confidently stated he could handle the outlaws of El Infierno. Right then he knew he'd have to stomach plenty. Gleeko had his own gang, five tough hombres. If he got rid of the sullen gunman he lost six guns, and risked dissension at the very onset of the campaign. Tight-lipped, he strode back to his pony, bent to loosen its cinches—and read grim humor in Red's brooding eyes. "Wal, what's so doggone funny?" he snapped.

"You are, feller," said the gunman softly.

"How come?"

"Yuh kin shade thet coyote tuh the draw and yuh let him live."

"I ain't killin' without cause."

"In yore boots, I'd hev beefed him back in El Infierno."

"It ain't my way."

Red's eroded features crinkled in silent mirth. "Oncet I had big ideas, like you, kid. But I learned, and you'll learn—the hard way."

After supper, the outlaws gathered around a campfire.

Bill tossed aside the butt of his cigarette, stood up. "Lissen!" He spoke loudly, above the mumble of voices. "The Lazy H lays five miles east. They's a crew of ten, maybe less, around the spread. At sunup we'll ride in on them. I wanta palaver with the boss. And get this! No shootin' till I give the word."

Gleeko's discontented rasp challenged him. "Sounds loco tuh me. Ain't this a range war? Le's hit 'em under the moon. Circle the joint, set a barn afire, smoke the bustards out and cut 'em down."

"Sure thing!" cut in his rheumy-eyed side-kick. "This ain't a prayer meetin'!"

Red's purr, deadly with menace, stilled approving chuckles. "The way I figger this hand, the gink who pays the fiddler calls the tune. Bill, here, done hired you lobos, and what he sez—goes. Ef any gent's got contrary notions, now's the time f'r him tuh git up on his hind laigs—and I'll set him back on his hunkers!"

Bill broke an uneasy silence. "I'm thankin' you, Red, but yuh got it wrong. Ef any gent don't see eye tuh eye with me, let him shut his trap—or slap leather, because I'm acomin' asmokin'." He addressed the band at large but he eyed the group around Gleeko. There was no answer to his challenge, except in their eyes.

"Nice work, feller!" grunted Red, as Bill sank down again. "Yuh'll do tuh ride the river with!"

Lady Luck smiled on the renegades when they rode east at sunup. Chris Hansen's spread nestled in the hills, which made it a cinch to approach unseen. When Bill, with six riders trailing him, emerged from a brushy draw, a stone's throw from the huddle of buildings, there was no sign of opposition. Smoke rose in a straight column from the stovepipe chimney of the cookshack and ponies drifted around the corral.

The Boxed T boss had divided his force. Red had angled off with another contingent to ride in from the south, and Gleeko with his gang was circling to hit the spread from the east. Bill had allotted the bitter-faced man the longest ride, figuring he might start trouble, and the longer he was kept out of the picture the better.

A heavy-set cowman with stolid features lumbered out of a small frame shack as Bill and his party jingled into the yard. Hansen bellowed like a bull, and startled punchers poured from the cookshack, their jaws still working on chow. At sight of the compact bunch of heavily armed men, some punchers slid toward the bunkhouse to pick up their hardware. Others backed against the cookhouse wall, waiting uncertainly for word from their boss. It was obvious that the Lazy H had been caught "with its pants down."

Bill pulled away from his riders, walked his pony up to Hansen. The stolid cowman stood rasping his chin by the shack, eyeing the strangers in perplexity.

"Howdy!" greeted Bill. "I'm Carson, from the Boxed T."

"Wal, git tuh hell off my range."

"It ain't thet easy, Hansen."

"Yuh'll be damned uneasy ef yuh don't skeedaddle afore my boys dust off yore pants," blustered the other. From the corner of his eye, Bill glimpsed men sliding out of the bunkhouse, hastily buckling on gunbelts.

"We kin talk this over, peaceable," he urged, with an inward prayer that no excitable waddy would loose lead.

"Ain't nothin' tuh talk over," declared Hansen, heavily. "I'm havin' no truck with the Boxed T. Git yore lobos outta here, afore we fill yuh as full of holes as a sieve." He swung ponderously at the clatter of hooves, and Bill's lips quirked at the bafflement mirrorred upon his features as Red swept around the house with his riders. A warning shout from an observant cowhand pulled his head eastward, to sight Gleeko's gang approaching at a fast canter.

"Hell and blazes! Jim Thompson hire an army?" he ejaculated.

"Most," grinned Bill, "yuh ain't seen nothin' yet." His voice hardened, "Do we palaver, or do my boys smoke up the spread? Talk fast, Hansen!"

The cowman groaned as he took stock of the raiders. No need for this blocky young stranger to threaten. He could see at a glance that this force of bleak-eyed riders would wipe out his crew in minutes. And he had thought that the Boxed T, short-handed and ringed by enemies, had holed up in the home spread and was awaiting extinction! "Wal, what's yore proposition?" he growled.

"First, yuh git yore waddies into the bunkhouse. My boys are itchin' tuh pull trigger."

Hansen hesitated, gulped as Gleeko's bunch, ever spectacular, whooped into the yard at full gallop. He roared orders at his crew. Reluctantly, they moved toward the bunkhouse. Bill waited until the last man was inside, then breathed more easily.

"Wall, I'm lissenin'!" blurted the cowman.

"Pull outta this fracas and keep off Boxed T range," came back Bill promptly.

Hansen fingered his unshaven chin, frowning perplexity. Bill could almost read his thoughts. He had thrown in with the other Valley spreads against the Boxed T, probably sworn to stick until Thompson was through. Now, like a frog on a red-hot stove, he was burnt whichever way he jumped.

"Think fast!" rapped out Bill.

The burly cowman fidgeted in agony of spirit. "Gordamit, Carson, I ain't got no choice."

"Gimme yore word yore through," persisted his inquisitor inexorably, "or we make a bonfire of this spread."

The grizzled Hansen eyed his barns, bunkhouse, corrals, the fruit of a lifetime of toil, glared at the massed renegades. "I'm through—blast yuh—and the Lazy H u'll stink the length of the Valley!"

"Yuh got good sense," returned Bill evenly. "Yuh break yore word and I swear there won't be nothin' left of the Lazy H, outside of yore headstone. So long!" He wheeled his pony and rejoined the bunch. "Le's ride!" he said shortly.

"Tuh another prayer meetin'?" gibed Gleeko.

"Ef I say so—yep!"

Again they hit eastward, out of the hills on to a far-flung expanse of grama. Bill was jubilant over his success at the Lazy H. Hansen was an old-timer, slow-thinking and bullheaded, but his word was good. If guns had blared, the renegades would have wiped out the Lazy H crew, but he would have lost men, valuable men, and he needed every gun for the real showdown with Pancho Hernandez and the three north valley outfits.

They descended on the Frying Pan like a cyclone. It was a small spread—a long, low adobe, barn and corrals set out on the flats, near the shrinking pools of Lost River. But there was plenty water in the long tanks and the buildings were painted a dazzling white. The horseflesh in a fenced pasture brought envious glints to the eyes of the wild bunch as they swept past. Thundering in the lead, Bill caught sight of a puncher scurrying like a rabbit behind the barn, then sighted a red-cheeked, robust young fellow, in fancy silk shirt and tailor-made riding breeches, sprawled in a rocker beneath a wooden canopy built along the front of the adobe. A newspaper and a jar of tobacco sat on a table beside him. He eyed the milling mob of horsemen with faint curiosity, and raised a languid arm in salutation.

Bill stepped down, as did the bulk of his followers. Trailing their reins, they hit for the welcome shade of the canopy, hunkered against the house like a long row of close-packed buzzards, and rolled cigarettes.

"You the Smith jasper?" inquired Bill.

"Willoughby Chaucer-Smyth," corrected the Englishman, coolly appraising his visitor, "and whom might I be addressing?"

"Bill Carson of the Boxed T, and we don't crave trouble."

The Englishman smiled amiably and waved at a near-by seat. "Rest your bones, old boy! Why should I make trouble? There are six men on this beastly ranch and three are out in the great beyond. What is this—a social call?" He waved indulgently at the renegades, "I have never seen a more ruffianly crew."

"They kin shoot straight," said Bill shortly.

"I don't doubt it, old chap, for a moment." He eyed the row of sun-burnt faces with interest. "Externally quite forbidding, but undoubtedly sterling fellows at heart."

"Yuh throw in with Pancho Hernandez and his gang?"

"Decidedly not, old bean. Count me strictly neutral. The cow kings may battle, but Chaucer-Smyth remains aloof."

"Stay out and yuh'll side-step plenty trouble," advised Bill curtly.

"With pleasure!" returned the Englishman blandly. "A schoolboy jingle leaps to mind, 'Never trouble trouble 'til trouble troubles you.' Neat, what?" He rose and stretched lazily. "Don't hurry away! I should have at least one bottle of Scotch left, if my rascally employees haven't discovered it."

Red's shoulders shook with his peculiar silent laugh, as the Frying Pan owner jauntily entered the adobe. "I gamble thet dood would spit in the devil's eye. Watch him, kid, he's dangerous!"

"He don't even pack a gun!"

"Nope!" agreed the gunman softly.

Willoughby Chaucer-Smyth returned, a bottle beneath his right arm, glasses in one hand and a deck of cards in the other. He set the glasses on the table, dropped the playing cards carelessly beside them and extracted the cork from the bottle.

Gleeko, who never seemed to be far distant, grabbed the bottle and took a long drink. Red eyed Bill obliquely, but the Boxed T boss said nothing. He needed those six guns too badly to start trouble over a drink.

The bottle passed from hand to hand and emptied fast. Gleeko picked up the deck of cards, riffled them absently. "Yuh play poker, Limey?"

The Englishmen smiled modestly, "Out West one acquires the rudiments, y'know."

"Hey, boys!" yelled the renegade. "Who craves tuh set in a game?" A chorus of delighted yells and a stampede for the table answered him. Hilariously, men dashed into the house, packed out boxes and straight-backed chairs. In a trice, the table was ringed with close-set seats. At a fierce low-whispered word from

Gleeko, a lantern-jawed gunman unwillingly relinquished his seat to the Englishman.

The latter sat down and beamed around the expectant circle. "Shall we cut for deal?" he inquired genially, and fished a fat roll of currency from a hip pocket. Gleeko licked his lips.

"Wal?" purred Red, as Bill stood back, ignored and forgotten.

"Let 'em play awhiles," said the young leader carelessly. "The Boxed T ain't more than three hours' ride." His plans were rolling as smoothly as a well-greased wagon wheel. It would be time aplenty if he made his triumphal entry into the Boxed T in the cool of evening.

Red slithered away and joined the onlookers, wedged three-deep around the card table. Bill eyed the Englishman's ruddy, smooth-shaven features, wreathed in innocent content, then glanced at the bronzed, hawklike faces of his fellow players. A dove, he thought pityingly, would have a better chance against a flock of black buzzards.

The sun dropped behind the distant Dragoons, when the bunch, again jogging northward, came in sight of the fortlike Boxed T. Bill turned toward Red and saw that the gunman's shoulders quivered with inward mirth.

"Wal, what in heck's got into yuh now?" he demanded.

"I jest cain't ferget thet doggoned Limejuicer, innercent as a day-old calf, cleaning out Gleeko and the card-sharks. 'Member I told yuh he was dangerous? I kin read signs. I gamble Gleeko's sore enough tuh chew nails."

"The Limey was jest lucky."

"Lucky!" Again Red was convulsed with silent laughter. "Every holdup man don't pack a hoglaig. He sets out a deck of cards and pulls out a roll yuh could choke a hawse with. Hell, thet was a come-on trick when I wore three-cornered pants."

"Fergit the Limey!" grunted Bill. "Thet's the Boxed T ahead."

Red squinted through the gathering purple at the square-built massive ranch house. "They's a lookout on the roof," he volunteered. “Sun flashed on metal. Reckon they lamped our dust way back.”

Steadily, the cavalcade jogged on. The buildings grew plain, but the grim adobe, silent and forbidding, might well have been deserted. Sudden uneasiness seized Bill. They were close enough now to sight rifle barrels protruding from the slit windows and the apertures along the low roof parapet. Their leader’s uneasiness spread quickly among the renegades. Taut silence cloaked them. A thought hit Bill like a bullet—maybe Pancho had struck again, cleaned up the Boxed T crew and taken over the spread. Confirming his fears, a gunflash bloomed luminous at a window and the slug zipped into the dust.

CHAPTER TWELVE

AT SIGHT OF THE SUDDEN RIFLE FLASH from the fortlike ranch house, the renegades pulled rein as one man. Angered curses from the astounded riders, bunched behind him, crackled upon Bill's ears, as he eyed the Boxed T in puzzled dismay. Again, two—three lances of flame licked from the slit windows and lead droned viciously through the still air.

Bill whirled his pony. At a canter, he led his followers back until they were well beyond rifle range. A barrage of barbed comment hit him when he again checked the dun and the bewildered renegades circled their ponies around him.

"What kinda sandy yuh runnin', mister?" flung Gleeko. "Warn't we hired tuh side the Boxed T? What kind of a boss are yuh when they say hello with lead?"

"If the sign reads right," said Bill tightly, "there ain't no Boxed T. 'Pears like Pancho done cleaned up and took over. We got a real job on our hands."

"Wal, I ain't—" began the bandit sourly, but Red's purr cut him short. "Yuh ain't doin' nothin', bud, but hobble yore lip, while we figger this out." He kneed his pony up to Bill's stirrup. "Le's take a pasear, feller!"

Again the two walked their ponies toward the ranch, while the renegades sat their mounts, watching in confused uncertainty.

"How long since yuh rode outta heah?" inquired Red.

"Three days, I guess."

"Leave any guns tuh hold the spread?"

"Yep, twenty or more."

"And they figgered yuh'd be back with a bunch tuh side 'em?"

For a moment Bill was silent. The gunman's questions had touched off a new train of thought. There was a simple explanation for the hostile reception—too simple," he thought wryly.

"The boys wouldn't know I was ridin' in with more guns," he confessed. "I dropped below the Border on a hunch."

"Hell, kid, in this light, how would yore boys, expectin' trouble, read our brand? F'r all they know, we might be thet Pancho outfit, packin' trouble."

"The same idea jest struck me," rejoined Bill quickly. Hope shot a feeble ray of light through the thick cloud of disappointment that fogged his mind.

"Pull rein, I'm ridin' ahead."

"Hold it!" Red's arm darted out. He grabbed the dun's headstall. "Yore stakin' yore life agenst a hunch."

"The odds suit me!" came back Bill shortly.

"Yore playin' the hand," said the gunman indifferently. He loosed the headstall and reined in. Bill kneed his dun to a trot. Right arm held high, palm extended, he jogged closer and closer to the silent, somber spread. Bunched in his rear, a dark blotch of riders watched his solitary advance, threw wagers around as to how far he would ride before he was knocked out of the saddle. Gleeko offered to lay twenty against ten he would never reach the ranch. Red drifted back in time to take the bet.

Quickly, the ranch house bulked larger as Bill steadily moved forward. There was no sign of further action. The very stillness was menacing. Soon he was close enough to focus the slit windows, bristling with guns. If he'd guessed wrong, he thought with fatalistic calm, he was through. They'd fill him so full of lead he'd sink in brine before he could wheel his pony.

The massive plank door of the ranch slowly swung open and a tall, stringy rider stepped out. Bill almost yelled his relief. There was only one Fiddlefoot. No one could mistake that beanstalk who ducked his head to avoid hitting the doorway.

He released a yippee and roweled the pony as he hurtled toward the tall man.

"Say, what's the big idea, throwin' lead at yore own pards?" he demanded, yanking the pony to a sliding halt.

"B'gawd, Bill," roared Fiddlefoot, "yore a sigh f'r sore eyes. Some claimed yuh'd beat it. I figgered yuh was buzzard bait." He nodded across the flats. "Whar in the name of creation did yuh corral thet bunch yonder? We had 'em tallied as Pancho's wolves."

"Nineteen hombres," announced Bill proudly, "and every one tough enough tuh chew cactus. All on the Boxed T pay roll!"

The bean pole twirled a drooping tip of his sun-bleached mustache, grinned at the exhilaration in Bill's voice. "And I thought the age of miracles was past," he murmured. "Come on in, Bill. I'll send a man out tuh bring in yore pards. Jim Thompson u'll be so doggoned tickled when he gits a load of this he's liable tuh sprout wings and fly."

Pegleg, the cook, had thrown together a quick meal for the renegades and they had settled down in the bunkhouse. Bill relaxed in a straight-backed chair beside Thompson's bed and told of the ambushing of the Boxed T punchers, his trip to El Infierno and the descent of the renegades upon the Lazy H and Frying Pan.

The cowman's deep-set eyes never left Bill's face as he listened. At the end of the rider's terse rcital, Thompson turnd his head toward Fiddlefoot, towering on the other side of the bed. His blue eyes were bright. "Thet's ten cart wheels yuh owe me, yuh doggoned desert canary," he chortled. " 'Member yuh claimed Bill had curled up? Dammit, I *knew* he'd come through."

"Aw right, boss, yuh don't hev tuh rub it in," grinned Fiddlefoot. "Bill faded and I figgered him daid. I knew he warn't so scared he back-trailed f'r Texas, like Pete claimed."

"Not Pete Lastro!" Bill almost shouted.

"The same," rumbled Fiddlefoot. "Pete bust inter the spread around midnight. Told as how Pancho had bushwhacked the boys at the ford outside Painted Rock. Seems Pete spurred ahaid and rode through. Lady Luck shore rode with him, warn't another jasper got clear. Baldy checked out next day."

Bill pondered upon this surprising information with puckered brow. At length, he inquired shortly, "Lastro git his job back?"

"Shore!"

The chunky rider rose abruptly, jaw set, "I'm through, Thompson!"

"Hey, they's no call tuh take the bit in yore teeth, son!" The cowman eyed him keenly. "How come yore on the prod so almighty sudden?"

"I gotta hunch Lastro's in cahoots with Pancho. Every pore bustard at the ford was filled with lead, and I mean filled. All save Lastro—and he's not scratched. It don't make sense tuh me."

Fiddlefoot and the old cowman exchanged glances. The gleam in the tall rider's eyes plainly said, "I told yuh so!"

Thompson snorted, again directed his attention to the belligerent Bill, "I reckon yuh and Pete don't see eye to eye, son, but yuh got no right tuh claim he's crooked."

"He's so doggoned crooked he'd swallow nails and spit out corkscrews," reiterated Bill obstinately.

Thompson's eyes froze with anger. He caught Fiddlefoot's mocking gaze and his square-hewn features relaxed. "How would yuh handle it, Bill?" he inquired mildly.

"I'd boot Lastro off this spread tuh hell and gone," retorted Bill vehemently.

There was a pause. Bill could have sworn Fiddlefoot was choking with inward laughter.

"Go ahaid!" said the cowman slowly. "Yore the boss!"

Mollified, Bill dropped back to his seat. "Yuh heard from Pancho?"

"Wal," returned Fiddlefoot, with a comical glance at the bedridden cowman, "we heard plenty of him. Afore we pulled the boys in, his doggoned vaqueros beefed two at Still Water, and right now I guess he rides herd on everything beyond the river."

"At sunup," said Bill decidedly, "we are goin' way beyond the river. There's nothin' I crave more than tuh get at thet Mex."

"Pussonel?" inquired the tall rider.

"Yuh bet yore life!" Bill loosened the bandana, gathered high around his neck. Fiddlefoot whistled low at sight of the deep-cut red weal.

The Boxed T bunkhouse was as crowded as a saloon on payday. At the table, a couple of poker games were going full blast. A bottle was circulating at a third game, where a group gathered around a blanket spread on the floor. The long, bunked-lined room was thick with men, some hunched in talk, others cleaning guns, mending or just loafing. One callow puncher devoutly studied a tattered mail-order catalogue. When Bill stepped in, the deep drone of voices reminded him of swarming bees. Maybe, he thought whimsically, hornets might be a better description.

Momentarily, misgiving seized the young boss as he gazed through the blue haze of tobacco smoke at the thronged men. Most of these hard-bitten hombres were packing guns when he was packing books to school. They had cut their eye teeth on gun sights and the butts of their sixes were notched aplenty. And he, who had never killed a man until he rode into Grass Valley, had the gall to think he could handle them and lead them against three embittered spreads. Hesitantly standing in the doorway, ignored and unnoticed, he caught sight of Red, brooding alone, like a battered eagle. The gunman's restless eyes flicked over him and Bill read cynical mockery in their depths. It seemed that this soft-voiced two-gun man was reading his very mind. Damn them all, he thought savagely. He might lack years but he could shade every man in that bunkhouse, excepting maybe Red. He was the son of Lightning Lefevre and Lightning was once kingpin of the Border. What in heck had he to be scared of?

He elbowed down the room, lifted a horseshoe off a peg over a bunk and banged it loudly on the table. The steady rumble of sound broke. Forty pairs of eyes focused him. "Lissen," he announced loudly, "at sunup, Fiddlefoot will pick a dozen hombres tuh hold the ranch. I'm takin' what's left tuh smoke out Pancho Hernandez—and it won't be a prayer meetin' this time!"

"Say, Carson, ain't yuh forgot I'm around heah?" Pete Lastro heaved from the group of card players at the further end of the bunkhouse. Boiling mad, the burly foreman strode down the room, shouldering men heedlessly aside. Close set above his broken nose, his eyes were bleary. As he neared the table, he hitched up his gunbelt. Carried enough booze to drown his good sense and make him pecky, registered Bill.

Quick to scent trouble, men broke to right and left like startled quail, flattening against the side-wall bunks. In seconds, the center of the room was clear, except for Bill's blocky form by the table, littered with hastily abandoned playing cards, and Lastro, ponderously advancing.

Six paces distant, the crooked-nosed foreman stopped. "Wal," he rasped, "who's dishin' out the orders around heah?"

"Not you, yuh double-crossin' bustard," came back Bill evenly. "Yore fired—right now!"

"And who give yuh the right tuh fire me—yuh ring-necked little rooster?" demanded the foreman thickly.

"Yore fired! Now put up or shut up!" Bill's voice was embit tered by the thought of ten dead men.

Brittle silence held the close-packed bunkhouse, a silence born of the certainty that Death was hovering close and at least one man was about to join his grisly company. If either of the two who faced each other in the center of the room backed water now, he would be branded yellow as long as he lived.

The whistle of Lastro's quick indrawn breath was loud in the ears of the expectant men. Bill had stepped away from the table and stood, alert and relaxed, arms hanging limp. He had no great respect for the big foreman's gun speed, and he had a deep-seated contempt for a traitor.

Boots crunched on the gravel outside, plain in the silence. Bill remembered one of Crawler's gun tricks. As though alarmed by the sound, he half turned, swinging away from his opponent. Instantly, Lastro dabbed for his gun.

Almost contemptuously, Bill's left hand flicked down. A slug ripped through the foreman's thick wrist. His iron clattered to the floor and blood spurted scarlet upon it. Grunting with pain, Lastro snatched off his bandana and awkwardly wrapped it around the wound. Bill watched him through the swirling gunsmoke. "Beat it!" he advised wearily. "A feller as slow as you shouldn't pack a gun."

"Not when yore around," rumbled Fiddlefoot's deep voice from the doorway. "Goshdarnit, Bill, whenever I see you, I smell gunsmoke."

Tension relaxed in a flood of talk. Bill dropped down beside Red and rolled a smoke. Cursing, as the numbness left his wrist and the pain in his arm grew, Lastro shambled outside. A waddy threw his soogans together, spooled them hastily and hurried after the ex-foreman. Silently, Red straightened and slid out behind them.

After a while, the gunman drifted back and hunkered beside Bill again. "Who's the skirt around heah?" he purred.

"Thompson's daughter."

"Friendly with thet jasper yuh jest winged?"

"Mebbe."

Red laughed silently. "There ain't no mebbe. I been coyotin' around. They had quite a confab behind the house. She give him a note, f'r Pancho."

"The hell yuh say!" ejaculated Bill incredulously.

"Yuh heard me!" came back Red softly. "And ain't yuh fergot? Lastro u'll wise up the spig thet yore on the warpath."

"Shore," returned Bill absently, "I figgered on thet." But his thoughts revolved around Mildred Thompson. Why would the cowman's daughter send a message to Pancho—her paw's deadliest enemy?

CHAPTER THIRTEEN

BEFORE THE RISING SUN cleared the Pinalinos, twenty-eight heavily-armed riders splashed across the Lost River behind Bill Carson. Plenty enough, he thought pridefully, to call Pancho's hand and clean up Boxed T range. Siding him was Cherokee, a squat, saddle-worn puncher who knew every canyon and arroyo in the Valley.

Across the stream, Bill followed the wagon road that curved east toward Painted Rock. Cherokee pulled over to his stirrup, "We gotta ride north, boss," he volunteered. "The P/H sets in the foothills.

"I changed my ideas," said Bill briefly. "We'll let Pancho set f'r a while. Right now I'm headin' f'r the Rocking T. Figger on dropping in, unexpected." It was plain, he decided, that Lastro would have ridden into Pancho's spread during the night, bursting with news of the Boxed T's new recruits and the impending attack at dawn. Three ranches lay at the northern end of the Valley, all declared enemies of the Boxed T—Pancho's P/H on the outskirts of the Black Hills; the Circle S, set midway across the Valley, and the Rocking T, due north of Painted Rock. In all, they mustered thirty-five riders. Chances were that Pancho, with no more than a dozen vaqueros to back his play, would yell for help at the threat of attack by a big force of Boxed T fighting men. The other two outfits would rush every last man to the P/H.

While they were forted up in Pancho's spread, reasoned Bill, awaiting attack, he'd have a mighty good chance to go on the rampage and clean up the two weakened ranches.

When Painted Rock took shape in the shadow of the square butte, a thought impelled him to speed Cherokee and two other Boxed T punchers ahead, with orders to circle the town and watch the stage road north. If a Circle S or Rocking T waddy should chance to be in town, sight the big Boxed T contingent and get away with the news, all chances of a surprise attack would collapse like an empty sack.

Painted Rock awoke abruptly when the menacing band of bleakfaced riders jingled into town. Uneasy citizens cat-toed along the plankwalks and seraped Mexicans slunk into alleyways. With ten miles of dusty trail behind them, the Boxed T gunnies wheeled to the hitch rails and swarmed joyfully into The Highway to Hell and Last Chance. Bill was in no hurry. The Rocking T lay less than an hour's jaunt north on the Deever stage road, and he planned to give Pancho's allies plenty time to ride westward to the Black Hills. A show of strength, too, in Painted Rock would do no harm; the Boxed T's waning prestige could stand a boost.

Jack Goodmer, the town marshal, lounged beneath the awning that shaded the rough rock front of the Grass Valley Bank, thumbs hooked in his belt, gray eyes taking stock of the strangers. Without apparent purpose, he idled along the hitch rails, reading brands on the sweated ponies, then dropped into The Highway to Hell, where Bill, Red and a dozen other gunnies were washing the trail dust out of their throats.

"Kinda expensive bunch of boys you hired," he commented affably, draping his lank form across the bar beside the Boxed T boss.

"Yuh can't hire gunhands f'r thirty and found," grunted Bill.

Goodmer smiled stonily. "Thet ain't exactly what I was drivin' at. Le's mosey down tuh the office."

Bill sensed hostility in the red-haired marshal's voice, swallowed his drink and tailed Goodmer through the batwings. Without further word, the lean marshal hit for his shack.

Bill watched curiously as the lawman yanked up a chair to the table that served him as desk, slid open a drawer and scooped up a double handful of reward notices. Quickly, he leafed through them, pausing occasionally to toss one out. When a dozen or more had accumulated, he looked up. "Git me, Carson? I gamble there's twenty thousand in bounty money ratholin' drinks downstreet."

The chunky rider nodded briefly as light broke upon him. He picked up the topmost dodger. From it, stared Gleeko's sour features. He read:

$1,000 REWARD

Wanted for Bank Robbery

Tony Gleikardi, alias Gleeko, alias Tony the Greek. Age 35; height 5' 11"; weight 165 lbs. Black hair, dark eyes. Bullet scar right forearm. Wanted for robbery with violence, Glenn County Bank, National Bank of Hargrove, Cattlemen's Bank, Saltmarsh, and theft of $34,000, gold and currency. Dangerous gunman. Heads Gleeko gang. 25% will be paid for all loot recovered.

John Masters, Sheriff,
Glenn County, Texas

Thoughtfully, Bill passed on to the others. All were among his recent recruits from El Infierno. His lips quirked as he met the marshal's accusing eyes. "Thet's all I could get," he exclaimed gravely, "there warn't any more!" And he told of his trip over the Border.

"Kin yuh handle 'em?" queried Goodmer dryly. "Ef them lobos git out of hand, they're liable tuh smoke up the town."

Bill shrugged. The preacher had asked the same question. Seemed like his lack of years told against him.

"Wal, chew on this," continued Goodmer tightly. "Yuh bring 'em into town agen and I'll arrest 'em, ef I have tuh deputize every man in the Valley. Yuh keep yore feudin' out on the range, we don't stomach gun wolves in Painted Rock. And yuh kin hightail jest as fast as yuh want. Right now wouldn't be too soon."

"There's no call tuh go on the prod," offered Bill placatingly. "We'll rattle our hocks, jest as soon as we get through lubricatin'. Yuh ain't fergot Pancho bushwhacked ten Boxed T boys hereabouts?"

"I ain't fergot my job is tuh keep order in Painted Rock. Yuh herd yore hard cases outta town, or the law u'll take a hand in this range war," decreed Goodmer firmly.

"We'll drift, pronto," promised Bill.

Light steps pattered outside and the shapely form of the marshal's vibrant sister hurtled breathlessly through the doorway, coppery hair aglint in the sun. She flashed a quick glance at the litter of reward notices and grinned impudently at Bill, "Looking over the family portraits, Mister Two-gun Man?"

"Yore brother saved me the chore," smiled Bill. "Ain't yuh scairt, with all these miscreants around?"

"Not when Jack's town marshal," she came back promptly. "Well, you'll need them all, to beat Pancho."

Bill stiffened. "We'll handle Pancho," he growled.

"Yes—boss!" she teased. "A little bird told me Pancho handled—you. Well, I really chased in to inquire why you never pick up your mail. A letter's been sitting in the rack at the post office for a week."

"Not for me!" said Bill promptly.

"It's addressed, Bill Carson. Of course, you may have foully murdered the real Bill Carson and assumed his name."

"Don't let Tess git yore goat," grunted the marshal. "She's a great little kidder. Not two days back I heard her upholdin' the Boxed T agenst a fistful of Circle S waddies, and she shore give yuh a build-up, feller."

"Don't flatter the man, his hatband's tight already," bantered the girl, but her cheeks flushed, "So long!" She bustled off with a careless wave of the hand, and the little office seemed suddenly dull and dingy to the Boxed T boss. His thoughts returned to the letter. Who would write him, outside of paw? And as far as he knew Crawler had never even learned to write. Maybe Tess Goodmer planted it, she had a mischievous gleam in her eyes.

Still doubtful, he clumped down to the Valley Merchandise Store, which handled everything from pins to plows. Two poke-bonnet women, fingering a bolt of calico, eyed him suspiciously as he squeezed past their ample forms, and several ancients, gathered around the cold stove, regarded him with interested speculation. With a start of surprise, he sighted a big black-bearded man in a rusty frock coat, half hidden by the huge, pot-bellied stove, nonchalantly dipping crackers out of a barrel.

Paul's deep voice boomed through the store, "I note that your journey bore good fruit, brother." He strode forward, brushing cracker crumbs from his beard. "You will observe that there is naught but poverty in the service of the Lord. Like the sparrow, I pick a mite here, a mite there. But my reward will come in Paradise." He focused the ancients with piercing gaze, "It is easier for a camel to pass through the eye of a needle than for a rich man to enter into the kingdom of heaven."

Bill stopped at the wicket. Sure enough, among the uncalled-for letters stuck in a rack on the wall was one addressed in crude, spidery writing to Bill Carson, Painted Rock, Arizona.

The postmistress, a prim little woman, stringy hair wound tightly around her head, smiled at the gaunt preacher. Her features tightened with severe disapproval, however, when she caught sight of Bill's two thonged-down guns.

"I reckon thet letter's f'r me, ma'am," he ventured.

"You have L.L. branded on your gun butts," she snapped.

Bill bit his lip, those gun butts were an eternal pest. The preacher sonorously solved his dilemma, "I, Paul, a humble servant of the Lord, will vouch for the young man, sister. He follows not the path of righteousness, but the Lord is ever merciful. There is hope yet for his immortal soul."

The good lady smirked, and released the mysterious letter. Paul sure had a way with the wimmen, thought Bill, with a tinge of envy. He tore open the gummed flap, extracted a folded sheet of cheap paper. Unconsciously, as he read the labored writing, slanted clumsily across the soiled sheet, he crushed the envelope in his fist, dropped it unheeded on the floor.

The message was from Crawler:

> You tangled yore spurs Bill? You shoulda rode back long afore this. Git Thompson pronto and git home. Burn this.
>
> Yore paw, Crawler.

Wrapt in thought, Bill moved over to the stove. Ignoring the old-timers' curious eyes, he set a match to the sheet and dropped it inside. The preacher stood back, intently watching.

The young rider headed for the street, pondering. In the excitement of battling for the Boxed T, he had almost forgotten his original mission. What a botch he had made of the job, he considered somberly. Paw had spent years drilling him in gun speed, for one purpose—to avenge a pair of crippled legs. And here he was fighting for the man he should have plugged. How could he ever make paw understand the jack pot he had gotten into from the start. How Thompson had saved his life twice, first from Pancho's vaqueros and then from Pete Lastro and the avenging Boxed T crew. Anyway, he had been forced to side the rancher or hang. He could imagine Crawler's lurid profanity if he voiced that alibi. Besides, he admitted uncomfortably, he'd had plenty chance to kill Thompson. He was just side-stepping the chore. Dammit, he *liked* the old rancher. He was no lousy bushkhacker, he just couldn't down Thompson unless the cowman drew on him. Maybe paw could kill in cold blood, but it just wasn't his way. Some time he'd have to ride back to Panther Gulch and face Crawler. What would he say, then? Preoccupied, Bill strode along the plankwalk. He'd forgotten the preacher. If he'd glanced back into the store he would have seen Paul unobtrusively kick the crumpled envelope behind a stack of brooms. Then bend casually to tuck his pant leg further into a high boot top and retrieve it. Balling the creased envelope in a bony fist, the preacher sauntered back to the cracker barrel behind the stove. Eagerly, he smoothed out the rectangle of paper, eyed the postmark. "San Andreas!" he murmured. "So thet's where Lefevre's skulked these many years—and men thought him dead! This day the Lord has been good to Paul, his humble servant."

With relief, citizens of Painted Rock saw the bleak band of Boxed T gun fighters head northward, following the stage road, deep-rutted by a decade of Concords and freight wagons.

A mile or more out of town, three waddies emerged from the brush.

"Ain't a jack rabbit passed this way," reported Cherokee.

Bill breathed deep with relief. "Keeno! You fellers hit f'r town and get yoreselves a snort, then ride hard f'r the Rocking T."

"That shore took a load off my mind," he confided to Red, as the three riders clattered away. The gunman laughed silently, swung around and pointed upward. Behind them towered the massive ramparts of the butte. From its square top, a thin tendril of smoke, like a dark thread, wound up into the blue. As Bill watched, the thread broke, balled into irregular puffs.

"Blanket signals. Some jasper's keeping cases on us right now," drawled Red, "and I gamble yore pard Pancho's got the low-down on our whereabouts."

Bill thought fast. The wily Mexican had outguessed him. He had taken it for granted that the butte could not be climbed. With a good pair of glasses, a lookout posted on those heights could command the entire north end of the Valley. The smoke signals would be visible as far as the Black Hills. It was a certainty that

Pancho knew they had side-stepped his spread and were raiding his neighbors. And it followed that the crews of the Rocking T and Circle S, who had been tolled to the Mexican's ranch, had been wised up, too. Would he have time to clean up on the two spreads before his opponents came streaking across the Valley? Maybe, he decided, if he moved fast.

"Shake it up!" he shouted, and set spurs to the dun. Quickly, he worked up from a trot to a canter, from a canter to a full gallop. The cavalcade strung out behind him, thinning as the slower ponies dropped behind. He checked his mount until a Boxed T puncher drew abreast. "Say, how far west is Pancho's layout?" he yelled.

The puncher opened and closed his left first three times, his voice lost in the thunder of hooves. Fifteen miles, considered Bill, that gave him less than an hour to act.

The band burned up a fast mile, then Bill reined the blowing dun dow nto a jog trot. For thirty minutes, the cavalcade drummed along the stage road, its youthful leader forcing the pace to the utmost. They breasted a low ridge and gazed down on the Rocking T buildings, grouped around a motionless windmill on the plain below.

Bill pulled rein, unbuckled a saddlebag and lifted out his glasses. While the stragglers rode in, he studied the ranch intently. There were few ponies in the corral and no other signs of life. He replaced the glasses, kneed the dun.

At a canter, the bunch jingled down the gentle slope behind him. Bill turned in the saddle, swung his left arm in a sweeping half circle. "Fan out!" he shouted. In a compact body his men made too good a mark, and who knew what awaited them at the apparently deserted ranch.

The men behind swung out on either side. Then, a long, uneven line of yelling men on madly racing ponies, they descended onto the Rocking T.

Three men could have handled the job, thought Bill, in disgust, instead of thirty. He stood by the water trough. Around him, the yard was packed with jubilant Boxed T riders. The bodies of two Rocking T waddies lay in the dust by the bunkhouse door. They had been unlucky enough to be left behind as a skeleton crew while their pards rode to reinforce Pancho. Awakened by the sudden rumble of hooves, they dashed outside—and crumbled before a leaden blizzard.

Bill's eyes wandered to the two lifeless gray-shirted figures. Needless killing sickened him, but how in heck could he stop it, he mused gloomily. How many more hard-working, loyal punchers would die before the ruckus was over, just because a few range hogs craved more land.

Impatiently, he indicated the barn. "Set a match to it," he directed shortly, "and lay off the rest of the spread. I got nothin' agenst these boys, 'cept they ganged up on Thompson."

"I'm gonna take a looksee in the house," announced Gleeko, swinging out of the saddle. "Mebbe they's some dinero cached around."

Bill stepped down briskly. He was getting mighty sick of the sullen-faced bandit and was in a mood for trouble. A few quick steps and he caught up with Gleeko, who was dodging through the tangle of riders. He reached forward and grabbed the taller man's arm. Gleeko whirled, eyes slitted, his right hand clamped on a gun butt.

"You step right back on thet cayuse," grated Bill, "or pull thet gun!"

Quick silence dropped on the riders around. This was the show down they had all been waiting for; the sour-faced bandit had been spitting like a wildcat ever since the band left El Infierno.

Gleeko dropped into a half crouch, thin lips drawn tight over his teeth. He glared into the younger man's blue eyes, cold and confident. Almost, it seemed, against his will, his fingers tightened on the gun butt—half drew it. The blocky young leader never moved—just watched him. Gleeko's nerve broke. With a quick oath he dropped his gun, pushed muttering past Bill toward his pony. For once, Red laughed—out loud.

The renegade stepped into the barn—backed out quickly. Beyond him, Bill saw loose straw crackle into a fierce blaze. Flames licked eagerly up the walls, tinder-dry, toward the rafters. A thin smoke haze stained the clear air.

Men pulled back as waves of heat beat out from the wide doorway. The air around them stirred, began to move in a steady draft toward the doomed building. The interior glowed red, was quickly transformed into a raging furnace. Gradually, the crackle of burning timbers was drowned by a deep, menacing roar as the fire took hold. Smoke rose thick now—a sullen column, tinged with a myriad sparks.

The yard was too hot for comfort. Bill gestured to Cherokee. "The Circle S!" he said curtly, when the rider pulled close.

They hit northwest, riding the swales that undulated like waves toward the shadowed hills. "Feller," said Red softly, "afore we hit the Boxed T agen, we'll git a bellyful." He jerked his head at the thick column of smoke, mushrooming high in their rear. "Ain't no mistakin' thet smoke signal."

CHAPTER FOURTEEN

PEACE LAY ON THE VAST CARPET of grama, rippling into the soft haze of distance, specked with grazing cows. Hock-high in grass, hoof-beats muffled, the raiders' ponies headed across the expanse toward the Circle S. There was no sign that death rode the range, except for the sullen column of smoke in their rear, slowly spreading like a pall, a black smear upon the blue sky.

Riding at the stirrup of the taciturn Cherokee, Bill dwelt upon what the next hour might bring. The lookout atop the butte behind Painted Rock had wrecked their plans. He had figured on making slashing attacks on the undefended Rocking T and Circle S, then circling into the hills and springing a surprise assault upon Pancho's spread before dawn. But now he had lost the advantage of surprise. Somewhere ahead was a force equaling or larger than his own, led by the wily Mexican. He would have given plenty to know just where Pancho was right then. He might be setting tight upon his spread, dashing to help defend the Circle S, or hiding out in the hills. Well, concluded the youthful Boxed T leader, a trifle grimly, he'd know about Pancho before many hours passed, and maybe the knowledge would be mighty unpleasant.

The Circle S sat serenely upon the flats, its buildings bathed in bright sunlight. As the Boxed T bunch drew close, Bill searched for sign of action, and saw none. Beyond the ranch stretched wave upon wave of low, barren hills, grayed with alkali dust, scabbed with broken rock. Arroyos ran down from the hills and gashed the plain, fingering to the very edge of the spread. A hundred men might lurk unseen in those arroyos, thought Bill, and it would take a full day to comb them out.

The grass thinned. Squatty greasewood, burnt brown by the sun, and thorny mesquite blotched the swales. Bill held his arm high and halted the column. Squinting beneath the brim of his Stetson, he eyed their objective, now scarcely more than a long rifle shot ahead.

The Circle S was another Boxed T, built on a smaller scale, but fortlike with slit windows and thick bulletproof adobe walls. Behind it, bunched bunkhouse, barns and corrals. There was not a pony in sight and the ranch lay as still as a tomb.

"What d'yuh make of it?" Bill turned to the silent Red.

"All set tuh say hello—with lead," returned the gunman, with a twisted grin. "They herded their saddle stock back inter the hills, outta trouble."

"Thet's how it strikes me. You take fifteen men, circle, fan out and injun in—there's plenty cover. When yore set, we'll hit 'em from the side."

Red nodded. Bill sat his pony and eyed the apparently deserted ranch while the gunman and his riders jingled off. The thought that he was overcautious intruded as Red's contingent cantered around the sleeping buildings and not a gun spoke. Seemed like they could have ridden right in and taken over. Plain in the clear air, Bill saw the other half of his force bunch on the far side of the ranch and step out of their saddles. Two riders led the ponies down the steep bank of an arroyo. As the ponies disappeared from view, Red's men, gripping their rifles, spaced out and began a cautious advance upon the ranch. The defenders, if there were any defenders, made no sign.

Bill was about to turn and signal the riders grouped behind him to ride in when a shot whiplashed the still air. One of the renegades beyond the ranch pitched forward upon his face and lay still. Before he hit earth, spluttering drumfire shattered the brooding silence, reverberating away into the hills. The ragged line of advancing renegades bellied down into the brush. The reports of their rifles mingled with the spiteful crackle of gunfire from the Circle S garrison. It was painfully apparent that this time the Boxed T raiders had tackled a nest of rattlesnakes.

Quickly, Bill swung out of the saddle and slid his Winchester out of the boot. The men behind him followed suit. Ponies were led back, and the party scattered. A belly-crawling advance upon the ranch commenced.

An hour later, the Boxed T bunch was still held at bay. Bill, flattened behind a low-growing shrub, empty shell cases thick beside him, paused to wipe the sweat and dust out of his eyes. The opening burst of gunfire had thinned out to intermittent sniping. Gophering around the ranch, the renegades threw lead spasmodically through the slit windows. In vicious reply, the defenders sprayed bullets whenever an attacker betrayed his position.

Seemed like they had hit a snag, the Boxed T leader thought wryly. If the Circle S crew had plenty ammunition, they could hold out for a week, two weeks. They were shooting from behind thick adobe walls, while his riders were hugging bare earth, with no cover beyond the brush. Red's party were snap-shooting from the outbuildings. It was clearly sheer suicide to attempt to rush the ranch by daylight, and by the time his renegades could crawl closer under the cloak of darkness, he might not have enough men left to attack. That lookout on the butte had sure set them in a jack pot.

Hoarse yells from the further side of the ranch interrupted his cogitations. The lazy gunfire suddenly whipped up into a frenzied crescendo. Surely Red was not loco enough to throw away men in a hopeless attack across the open yard, thought the perplexed Bill. Then he became aware that the brush around was agitated by moving bodies—his men were slinking back. Something was wrong, very wrong.

Joyous yippees resounded from the beleaguered Circle S and fire spurted from every window in the ranch. Lead lashed the brush as Bill squirmed around and swiftly wormed his way backward. To his right and left renegades slithered in full retreat. At last, out of range of the hammering rifles, Bill rose to his feet—and grasped the extent of the calamity that had overwhelmed his force. The hillside behind the ranch seemed alive with spitting rifles. Red and his men were hammered from front and rear, caught in a devastating cross fire. As Bill watched with sinking heart, the remnants of Red's force emerged from the arroyo, spurring madly to escape the hail of lead that tore into them. Less than a dozen in number, with several riderless ponies racing with them, they swept southward. Two, three men were pounded out of their saddles before they urged their desperately racing ponies clear of the corridor of fire.

The cause of the disaster was plain now to the stricken Boxed T leader—Pancho had hidden a force in the hills behind the Circle S, well knowing that the defenders of the ranch could beat off a daylight attack. Now he had thrown these reserves into action against Red's undefended rear.

Bill braced himself to meet the emergency. If the Circle S crew and Pancho's men joined forces, they might ride out and exterminate the remaining Boxed T raiders on the open plain.

Someone had signaled the horse tenders and the ponies came up at a gallop from the rear. The renegades swung eagerly into their saddles. Southward, Red and the survivors of his party were beating round to rejoin their pards. Bill led his men to meet them. They came together in a melee of blowing ponies and excited, cursing men.

"Guess we grabbed a bear by the tail!" No sign of panic showed upon Red's features, and there was more sardonic humor than alarm in his dry tones. "Reckon I left half my boys back there in the brush. How many yuh lost, Bill?"

"Three!"

"What's the play?"

"Split the breeze fore they ride us down."

Red shook his head, "They cain't, ain't a hoss around the spread."

Bill stared at the Circle S, squat and stubborn in the sunlight, and weighed the next move. A third of his force had been wiped out and he had gained nothing for the loss. With another bunch of riders loose in the hills and liable to launch a counter-attack at any moment, further siege of the Circle S was hopeless. He would be lucky to get his badly mauled force back to the shelter of the Boxed T. Pancho, forewarned by the lookout, had sure trumped his ace. But the blue-eyed Boxed T boss hated to slink back to the home spread like a beaten cur.

As he surveyed the ranch and the brown hills behind it, now apparently deserted, an idea hit him. If Pancho had concentrated his forces here, the P/H must have been left unguarded. Why not hightail for the Mexican's spread, put it to the torch and thus retrieve victory from defeat? Bill called Cherokee out of the press of angry, despondent riders.

"Where does the P/H lay?"

The puncher pointed south of the sun, now sinking toward the distant Dragoons. "Guess it's an hour's hard ride, boss, rough country."

Bill glanced again at the Circle S. There was no sign of an offensive; maybe Pancho's vaqueros were bringing the ponies in. "Le's ride!" he shouted.

A lone derisive shot echoed from the ranch as the repulsed raiders moved southward and headed into the labyrinth of hills.

An uneasy thought troubled Bill, tailing Cherokee, the guide. Pancho knew every canyon and cowpath at this end of the Valley. What if he guessed their purpose, cut ahead and ambushed them as he had the unlucky Boxed T punchers at the ford?

The Boxed T leader spurred abreast of the guide. "Say," he inquired anxiously, "could the bunch back at the Circle S cut ahead and bushwhack us?"

"Not unless they sprout wings," grunted the alkalied old waddy. "Lamp thet pass?" He indicated a notch in the barren chain of hills that looped across their front. From it, the terrain dropped down toward them in a series of lightly timbered benches. "Wal, there ain't no way a hawse could git tuh the P/H 'cept through thet gap, which is Coyote Pass. Ef we beat the bustards through there, it's a cinch. Pancho's layout ain't more'n four miles beyond."

Like a curling whip, the string of nodding ponies labored up toward the pass, ironshod hooves slipping and sliding on the steep, shale-covered trail. Apparently, there was no pursuit, but Bill did not breathe easily until they threaded through the narrow pass. Almost unscalable, steep slopes slanted upon either side, thick-studded with boulders that looked as though they would roll downward at a touch, and bare of vegetation except for a sprinkling of dwarf pine, rotted precariously in the crumbling earth. The trail itself was impassable to a wheeled vehicle and the ponies twisted like jack rabbits between huge fragments of rock that had spilled down the slopes.

Gleeko worked up to the front of the long, toiling column and braced Bill, "Figger them coyotes at the ranch u'll dog us, boss?"

"Wouldn't surprise me any."

"Wal, why don't yuh drop off a fistful of boys and bottle up the pass? Never seen a more likely spot."

Bill masked his surprise. Looked like the sour-faced bandit had undergone a sudden change of heart; all that he had contributed before had been snarling criticism. And Gleeko was right. Half a dozen men could hold the narrow, cliff-bound trail against a small army. "Yuh got somethin' there," admitted Bill cautiously.

"Me and my boys could handle it," came back Gleeko, off-hand.

Bill considered the offer in silence. If Pancho tailed them, and the odds were that he would, he would be compelled to ride through the pass. Three or four guns could block the trail as long as daylight lasted. What was more, this was the first helpful gesture Gleeko had ever made. It might be good business to encourage the hombre.

"Wal?" demanded the renegade, with a return of his former truculence.

"It's hunky-dory with me," agreed Bill. "If there's a fracas, pull out at sundown. Pancho's as clever as a coyote, and he'll burrow around after dark."

"Say, I was gun fightin' afore yuh was weaned!" came back Gleeko contemptuously. He reined off the trail and pulled his men out of the column as it filed past.

Red, whose questing eyes missed nothing, rode up to Bill when he saw Gleeko and his gang remain behind and peel out of leather. "What's cookin', kid?" he grunted, jerking his head backward.

Bill explained Gleeko's plan. "Sounds good tuh me," he concluded.

Red's saturnine features creased with mirthless laughter. "Nothin' Gleeko sez sounds good tuh me, thet hairpin's as crooked as a snake in a cactus patch. The buzzard's hatchin' up somethin'. Damned ef I kin figger what, unless he's sellin' out. Mebbe I should hev a word with the cuss." He neck-reined his pony around, jogged back to where Gleeko's gang grouped beside the twisted trail. Scenting trouble, Bill spurred after him. He sensed a deep-seated animosity between the two renegades.

The rheumy-eyed pard of Gleeko's stood apart, watching the back trail.

"What's on yore mind—greaser?" purred Red. The insulting epithet lingered upon his tongue as though he savored it.

The three men around Gleeko eased off as the bank robber stiffened. But he was careful to make no motion toward his gun. "The boss's wise, ask him!" he growled.

Bill rode between the two stormy-eyed men. "F'r gosh sakes, quit proddin', Red!" There was an edge to his voice. "Leave Gleeko hold the pass. Ain't we got plenty trouble without stirrin' up more?"

Red shrugged and wheeled his mount without further word. Reining around to follow, Bill glimpsed the rheumy-eyed rider crouched beside a boulder. Unobserved, he had drawn his gun and was deliberately lining the sights on Red's back. With the speed that years of practice had left as a legacy, Bill's right hand stabbed down. Even as the would-be murderer thumbed the hammer, a slug skewered his forearm. Deflected, his bullet zipped over Red's head. The soft-voiced bandit whipped around in the saddle, read the story at a glance. Before Bill could remonstrate, one of his triggerless guns was smoking, faster than a snake strikes. Pitilessly his lead hammered the wounded man against the boulder. Mouth agape drooling blood, the rheumy-eyed man slid down.

Brooding eyes flaming with fury, Red swung to face the remaining members of Gleeko's gang. His thin lips twisted in derision, "Wal, yuh lousy sheepherders, I still got three beans on the wheel."

Not a man moved.

Bill again eased his pony between the antagonists. "Le's go, Red!"

For a moment he read death in the gunman's slitted eyes, then Red's taut features creased in a mirthless grin. "Yuh got guts, feller!" He jerked his head toward the body of the dead man. "I won't ferget!"

Bill breathed deep in relief as Red touched his pony with the steel and jogged after the main body, now out of sight behind an outjutting shoulder of the pass.

In the graveyard watch, the lookout hunched on the flat roof of the Boxed T ranch house saw seventeen jaded riders ease their trail-worn ponies into the yard. Bone-weary, they stripped the gear off their mounts. Bill was rubbing down the dun with a gunny sack when Fiddlefoot's tall form loomed in the starlight. "Seems like I tallied thirty men when yuh rode out," he rumbled. "Ain't but seventeen rode in. Stub yore toe, Bill?"

"Yuh said it!" admitted the rider morosely. He tossed the sack to one side and loosed his pony in the corral. Fiddlefoot watched him, noting the droop of his shoulders and the flatness in his voice that bespoke fatigue.

With an effort, Bill set the pole gate in place, hunkered against the rail and built a smoke. The tall man jacknifed beside him. After a few draws, Bill told of the attacks on the Rocking T and Circle S. "We hit Pancho's spread last," he concluded with relish. "Rubbed out four vaqueros he'd left behind, put the torch tuh every building on the place, bar some adobes. Busted his water tank and scattered his saddle stock. And I ain't through yet—I aim tuh swing the greaser."

"The boys yuh left tuh block Coyote Pass shoulda been in afore this," observed Fiddlefoot thoughtfully.

"Oh, they'll drift along!" Bill rose, yawned. "Wal, me f'r the hay!"

Pegleg was gathering up the breakfast dishes, when the eyes of the riders saddling up around the corral gate opened wide as a shaggy mule ambled into view. Forking it was Paul the Preacher, long legs dangling and the tails of his rusty frock coat flapping like broken wings. He halted and stepped off, whereupon the mule headed for the water trough.

In no wise abashed by the silent scrutiny of many bleak eyes, Paul stroked his bushy beard and scanned them. "Greetings, brethren!" he boomed. "Ye may be sinners, but remember that there is more rejoicing in heaven over one sinner that repenteth than over ninety and nine just persons which need no repentance. Is one Bill Carson hereabouts?"

At that moment, Bill stepped out of the house, where he had been reporting the previous day's misadventures to the raptly attentive cowman.

Paul advanced to meet him. "I have tidings, grave tidings, brother," he announced.

"Gleeko?" inquired Bill, his voice shaded with anxiety, for the sour-faced bandit and his four men had failed to return.

"The same, brother. It is well if we talked alone."

Bill led the way into the empty cookshack, coaxed a mug of coffee out of the cook and set it before Paul.

He dropped on a bench beside the preacher. "Spill it!" he said resignedly. "My guess is thet Pancho cleaned up Gleeko and his boys."

Paul sipped his coffee with relish. "It were better if he had, brother. But they were well when I saw them in Painted Rock."

"What in heck they doin' in town?" demanded Bill, puzzled.

"That, brother, troubles me sorely—they are men of evil reputation."

Thought of the reward notice displaying Gleeko's sour features flashed into Bill's mind. Wanted on three counts of bank robbery! And there was nothing between Gleeko and his gang and the vault of the Grass Valley Bank but a lone town marshal!

CHAPTER FIFTEEN

GLEEKO'S TREACHERY was as plain as the ears on a mule, decided Bill, as he mulled over the preacher's warning. The sour-faced bandit had decided to quit the Boxed T pay roll after the repulse at the Circle S. By volunteering to guard the pass, he was able to cut out his gang without arousing suspicion. Probably, as soon as the Boxed T riders were out of sight, the five of them burnt up the trail to Painted Rock. If his past record meant anything, Gleeko was all set to hold up the Grass Valley Bank and streak for the Border. There was a chance, a mighty slim one, he could reach town before they pulled off the job. "Thanks, Preacher!" he jerked out. "I gotta move—fast." Before Paul had swallowed his second cup of coffee, Bill was hightailing for Painted Rock.

Nothing seemed amiss in town, when the Boxed T rider dropped his sweated dun down to a walk on Main Street. There was no sign of the bandits' ponies at the hitch rails and the saloons were empty of his quarry. Yet the questing rider felt that something was awry, though he could not place it. Not until he pulled up at the rail outside the town marshal's office did he realize what was wrong—no one was on the street, the town seemed as deserted as though a plague had struck it.

As he tied the dun, Bill glimpsed Jack Goodmer's face through the shack window. The marshal's intent gaze was focused across street—he was keeping cases on the bank, set on the opposite corner.

Bill ducked under the rail and stepped into the office.

"Howdy!" flung Goodmer absently, still gazing through the window.

"Yuh lamped any of my boys around town?"

"Yep—five of yore lily-white renegades, wanted f'r bank robbery."

"They ain't sprung the bank yet?"

"Nope," said Goodmer grimly. "Not yet!"

"Thank Gawd!" Bill dropped on to a chair, dabbed the dust and sweat from his face and neck. "They quit me—yesterday. The preacher put me wise they headed f'r town."

"We're all set tuh handle the rattlesnakes," grunted Goodmer, eyes never leaving the doors of the bank. "I got a dozen special deputies posted around, coverin' the bank. Yuh shore brought a swarm of tarantulas into the Valley, Carson." He paused, listened intently. "What in tarnation's broke loose downstreet?"

Both listened to a distant, confused shouting, fast growing more distinct. Then it was plain, as men flung the word, one to another, "Fire! Fire!"

"Hell!" groaned Goodmer. "This would happen—now!"

Together, they rushed outside. Fire was the eternal menace that hovered over every cow town. Few desert communities had adequate supplies of water beyond the little they used for immediate necessities; fewer had any fire-fighting apparatus, apart from bucket brigades and barrels set along the plankwalks. Once fire took hold of the heat-warped, tinder-dry building it was long odds that an entire town would be swiftly reduced to smouldering ashes.

Downstreet, smoke was plain, billowing from the rear of the close-packed, false-fronted stores. Like an anthill suddenly disturbed by an unwelcome intruder, Painted Rock came to life in a swirl of excitement. Storekeepers, clerks, barkeeps and Mexicans, toting buckets, axes, shovels, whatever first came to hand, scurried toward the conflagration.

Before Bill and the marshal had covered half the short distance to the outbreak, flames were wavering red above the false fronts and smoke-fogged Main Street. One building was already well afire and the whole block of sun-seared wooden structures seemed doomed. Beaten back by the heat and choking in the smoke-filled air, townsfolk gathered in flurried groups and watched the roaring blaze. Goodmer grabbed an excited townsman, "Whar did it start?"

"Lean-to, back of the saddler's, so they claim. B'gosh, Jack, the hull dang town's liable tuh be wiped out." He coughed as smoke eddied around them, hurried away.

Bill saw that two stores were now well alight and sparks were showering upon roofs of surrounding buildings. Men had abandoned all thought of checking the blaze. But hesitancy was gone; men, women and children became as busy as beavers, hauling goods and furniture out of doorways along the block. Queer, thought Bill, that fire should break out in midmorning, with Gleeko and his gang coyoting around. Then, like a lightning stroke, realization hit him—Gleeko had set the town afire to cover his holdup.

Bill swung around to Goodmer. "The bank!" he yelled. "Gleeko started this!"

At a run, the pair headed upstreet, panting through a black murk, out of which men appeared and disappeared like sooted ghosts. Guns commenced to boom ahead, the crack of Winchesters mingling with the deeper roar of forty-fives. A puff of wind momentarily cleared the street. Outside the Grass Valley Bank stood a rider, holding five saddled ponies. Four men burst out of the bank. Bill recognized Gleeko, packing a swollen gunny sack.

Several of Goodmer's deputies must have stuck to their posts; for guns were roaring across street. A bandit went down as the gang swung into their saddles. Two more were swept out of leather before they could whirl their ponies. Then, wantonly, the breeze shifted and thick smoke blacked out the picture. Bill had a blurred glimpse of the two surviving bandits spurring madly toward him, six guns winking through the haze. The running men were in the direct path of the hurtling riders. In a flash the racing ponies were upon them, looming gigantic in the smoke fog. Bill flung to one side, to escape the flailing hooves, stumbled and fell headlong. He picked himself out of the dust, flung lead at the rapidly disappearing horsemen. He heard the flat slap of a bullet against Goodmer's chest. The marshal staggered, clutched at his bloodied shirt and dropped. Again, the vagrant breeze swept aside the veil of smoke. The bandits were pounding down-street, out of range of a short gun. Goodmer's body was crumbled in the dust and Bill stood near by, a smoking gun in each fist.

The Boxed T rider flinched as lead droned past his ear. He became aware that slugs from the concealed deputies were kicking up spurts of dust around him. Shouts of alarm reached his ears as the bandits raced past the blazing buildings, triggering through the smoke flurries. A bullet plucked softly at his Stetson. He swore softly, cursing the deputies' misdirected shooting. A hammer blow pounded his forehead, a thousand sparks exploded before his eyes, consciousness fled as he dropped limply beside the town marshal's still form.

Bill awoke in semidarkness. His head felt as though he had been pole-axed. Struggling to organize his jumbled faculties, he fingered a thick bandage wound around his head and stared at a small square of bright light high above.

Gradually, recollection returned—the fire, Gleeko's raid on the bank, the smashing blow that downed him. Maybe another pony happened along and kicked him, he pondered. Still dazed, he sat up and looked around. His jaw dropped with astonishment—he was in a cell. There was no mistaking the steel bars, a bucket set in the corner, the bleak adobe walls scrawled with the names of former prisoners.

Repressing a groan, for every movement jarred his injured head, Bill dropped his legs over the edge of the bunk, swayed to his feet and moved uncertainly toward the barred cell gate.

In the dim light he eyed three other cells, all empty. There were four in all, two set on each side of a short, wide passageway. He clung to the steel gate with both hands and rattled it with all his strength. The jangle filled the jail, but no one came. From habit, he felt for his guns, but they were gone. He staggered back to the bunk and dropped upon it, sick in body and mind, wondering numbly what capricious stroke of fate threw him behind prison bars while Gleeko split the breeze for the Border with his loot.

The rattle of a key in the lock of the outside door brought his head up. A wizened old-timer, jaws champing on a chaw, a big Colt buckled above his hips, stepped into the jail. Behind him bulked a familiar figure, Paul the Preacher.

Bill sprang to his feet and advanced to the bars. "Say!" he demanded angrily. "What's the big idea? I don't belong here!"

"The way folks feel around town," came back the old-timer in a cracked voice, "yuh won't be heah long, no siree! They're fixin' tuh hang yuh up tuh dry."

"What in hell f'r?"

The jailor ejected a stream of tobacco juice and turned to the shaggy Paul. "His gang burns down half the danged town and busts inter the bank, and he axes why folks crave tuh stretch his neck," he cackled. "Ain't thet a lapaloozer?"

"Judge not that ye be not judged, with what measure ye mete it shall be meted unto you," intoned Paul. "You may leave, brother, I would save his immortal soul."

"Gotta lock yuh in, Parson," wheezed the ancient. "Thet hombre is plumb pizen. Be back in ten minutes. And stand clear of the rip-snortin' wildcat, he's liable tuh claw!" Chortling, he moved away and slammed the heavy outer door behind him.

"Say, Preacher, set me right or I'll go loco," implored the perplexed Bill. "How in heck did I come tuh be jugged?"

Paul stood close to the bars, stroking his black beard. "Have faith, brother, those whom the Lord loveth, he afflicteth. All will yet be well."

"How come I'm here?" reiterated Bill.

"Circumstances, brother. The ways of the Lord are inscrutable. Friend Goodmer posted deputies to watch the bank. Smoke from the fire set by those sons of Belial obscured their vision, for they swear that you shot the marshal and covered the getaway of your renegades." Bill remembered the deputies' lead spitting into the dust around him.

"Hell, I rode tuh town tuh warn Goodmer, yuh know thet!"

"He cannot testify on your behalf, brother, he lies at the very threshold of death. I have reasoned with them, in vain. When anger enters, justice flees; they are cruel with wrath and fierce anger. The vault of their bank is empty and much of their town in smoking ruins. They demand vengeance for their looted savings and gutted homes. There is talk of a lynching, brother."

"So I stopped a bullet!" Bill fingered the bandage around his head. "I figgered a horse kicked me."

"A mere graze, brother. Your skull is thick, for which the Lord be thanked."

Grating hinges on the outer door heralded the jailer's return.

"Say, I gotta get outta this," urged Bill. "They shoulda got a posse together and hit Gleeko's trail. If he reaches the Border they'll never see a dollar of thet loot again."

"Patience, brother, patience," boomed Paul. "Thy faith shall make thee whole—and a prayer would not be amiss. I like not the mood of the people. If Goodmer dies, naught but a miracle will avail you." With these somber words, he strode toward the outer door.

Again Bill sank upon his bunk and cogitated bitterly upon his luck. The error of the deputies was understandable. He was a stranger and a gunman. In their eyes, he led the renegades. Billowing smoke had obscured the getaway of Gleeko. When the breeze swept the smoke aside, he was standing beside the fallen marshal, holding a gun. His pony was tied close by. So they had jumped to the conclusion that he had shot Goodmer and was covering the fleeing bandits. How could he prove otherwise? Jack Goodmer was the only man who could clear him, and Goodmer was dying.

The small square of light dimmed as the day wore on. Nothing broke the prisoner's solitude as he hunched in the bare cell. Through the window, high on the wall, drifted the acrid smell of smouldering timbers and the sound of occasional distant shouting. But, as the day died, a new menace brought Bill apprehensively to his feet. Growing louder as the darkness thickened, the rumble of voices outside reached him. Ears intent, he could hear the shuffle of many feet; muted tones, deep and threatening. His shirt was clammy against his back as he visioned a mob gathering, grim and relentless, around the little adobe jail. It could be there for only one purpose—to exact vengeance upon the man who they believed had brought disaster upon Painted Rock.

The the brooding night was rent by a rumbling growl that swelled into a roar. Awesome in its animal ferocity, the savage tumult of sound crystallized into a savage chant, "Lynch him—lynch the bustard—lynch him!"

Caged and impotent, Bill paced his cell, fighting to control a rising panic, the like of which he had never known before. He could face death with calm fatalism, when he had a gun at his side and a fighting chance for survival. But this was different. Unarmed and alone, he was as helpless as a blind kitten in a den of wolf cubs. He sensed that the mob outside was as devoid of mercy as a pack of lobos. Those hoarsely chanting men were no longer tolerant, justice-loving human beings, but raging fanatics, bereft of reasoning power, swayed by blind passion; possessed of only one thought—revenge for loss of homes and savings; conscious of only one urge, to kill.

The outer door shivered before the impact of a heavy object. The chant ceased, and the expectant silence as the pack tensed to snatch its prey rasped like a rusty file upon the prisoner's tight-drawn nerves.

CHAPTER SIXTEEN

A SHRILL YELL ripped the ominous quiet, "Fire!" Back of the barbershop. Git yore buckets and hump yore tails or the rest of the town u'll go up in smoke!"

Tensed inside the jail, Bill heard the shouts of alarmed men, the dull pounding of many boots on the baked ground, then silence. He breathed deep in relief. Maybe one of the gutted buildings had flared up again. Well, it gave him another hour of life.

Magnified by the sudden quiet outside, the rasping of the gritty hinges on the outer door sounded loud in his ears. He could see nothing in the gloom of the ill-lighted cell, but his questioning gaze fastened on a bar of graying light that widened as the door was cautiously eased open. A blurred figure slipped through, the hinges complained again and the bar of light was gone.

Red's repressed tones galvanized the prisoner, "Hey, kid, whar yuh at?"

"Right ahead!" With difficulty, Bill restrained himself from yelling, as hope flooded through him.

A shadowy figure eased up to the barred cell gate. The lock clicked and the gate swung open. The gunman stepped into the cell. Two shotguns were tucked under one arm, and Bill's guns dangled from his left hand.

Eagerly, the prisoner buckled on his forty-four's. Red fished a handful of shotgun shells from a pants pocket and passed them over, together with a ten-gauge, double-barreled shotgun. "Le's beat it, kid!" he said laconically.

Together, they hit for the outer door. Red set his shoulder against the bolt-studded timbers, eased the door ajar and poked his head through the gap. "Hold it!" he warned softly. Bill, fretting at his heels, curbed his impatience. After a long pause, the gunman pulled back, gently closed the door, inserted a heavy key in the lock and shot the bolt home.

"Guess we're corralled," he told the perplexed Bill. Nonchalantly jerking the makin's out of a vest pocket, he commenced to build a smoke. "They's a bunch of salty gents out yonder keepin' cases on this canary cage. Musta lamped me moseyin' around."

"Hell, can't we blast through!" The prisoner's voice was heavy with disappointment.

"Nope, feller," came back Red firmly. "We're better off whar we are. This joint's bulletproof and fireproof. Set down and rest yore laigs!" He led the way back to Bill's cell, dropped onto the bunk and casually touched a match to his smoke.

"How come yore in town?" inquired Bill, morosely settling down beside him.

The gunman chuckled. "Jest a hunch. I lamped the preacher ride inter the spread and you ride out. Around noon I begin thinkin' of Gleeko and the bank—all ready tuh be picked, like a ripe melon. So I saddled up and headed thisaways. When I hit town, most of Main Street was smokin' ashes. Then I run acrost the preacher agen and got the low-down. Goodmer's sister, a spunky gal, done rode out tuh the Boxed T f'r help. I circulated around and scented trouble. When the boys started bustin' in the door I got busy—set a shack afire. Thet tolled 'em away. I dropped inter the marshal's office, gathered up the hardware and hotfooted it over heah. Reckon thet's about all."

Bill digested Red's laconic words in silence. So Tess rode for help, which proved she was convinced of his innocence. He was conscious of a quick uplift of spirits. When a fellow got in a jam like this he found out who his real pards were. And who would have thought that the man calmly smoking beside him, a hired gunman and a killer, would risk his life to ease a comparative stranger out of a jack pot—with no chance of gain? "Say Red," he urged, "yuh got no stake in this—beat it! They'll be back and we can't hold out overlong. No sense in two of us cashin' in. I'm sure mighty grateful f'r what yuh've done."

"Fergit it, feller!" yawned the gunman. "The boys from the ranch are liable tuh ride in most any time. With these babies," he patted the twin barrels of his shotgun, "we're in clover. 'Sides, remember the pass? I pay my debts!"

For a space they smoked in silence, the cigarette tips glowing like sparks in the darkness. Then again Bill heard men stirring outside. There was an impatient banging on the outer door. Muffled, a man's voice filtered through, "Hey, you inside! Bring out the scatter-guns and key's, or we'll string yuh up with thet lousy firebug."

Red crushed his smoke, rose. "Kid," he said softly, "Old Man Trouble's done arrived." He crossed the passageway and opened a cell door on the opposite side. Took up his station inside.

A heavy object crashed against the ironbound door. It trembled beneath the impact, but stood firm. A pause, then another thunderous impact. In the brief silence that followed, Red's sibilant whisper floated across the jail, "It won't be long now, kid!" Bill could have sworn that the saturnine gunman was laughing in his peculiar silent fashion.

A third smashing assault, the harsh squeal of metal wrenched from sun-shrunk timbers and the heavy door, torn off its hinges, slammed down. Framed in the faint rectangle of light which was the doorway, Bill saw a group of men, hefting a long, heavy balk of timber. Behind them, a blotch of onlookers.

A double explosion deafened him as Red loosed both barrels of his shotgun through the gap. A confusion of yells, shrieks and imprecations filled the air as the spreading buckshot ripped into the crowd. Like startled deer, the mob scattered. As if by magic, the stretch of weed-covered ground before the jail was cleared. The only reminder of the attack was the heavy battering-ram lying across the smashed door. “I reckon,” commented Red complacently, from a dark corner of his cell, “thet’ll sure enough hold ’em f’r a while.”

A bullet droned through the open doorway and flattened on the far wall. Close following, slugs buzzed into the jail like angry hornets, chipping the adobe walls and snarling in shrill ricochet off the steel-barred cells.

Crouched out of the line of fire, Bill waited. If the irate citizens of Painted Rock contented themselves with long-range shooting, he and Red could hold the thick-walled jail for a long, long time.

His satisfaction was short-lived. The interior of the jail was suddenly bathed in bright light as a flaming bundle of oil-soaked rags dropped down from the small window high above his head. Other blazing fireballs quickly followed. Bill yanked the straw mattress off his bunk and smothered those within reach, but others lay in view of the marksmen outside. Their assailants were screened by darkness, but every corner of the jail was brilliantly illuminated. When Bill tried to rake a flaming bundle toward him with the shotgun barrel, a continuous stream of bullets pecked at it. And more fireballs were dropping every minute.

From across the jail, Red blasted the small window through which they were pitched—without effect. It was plain that someone was standing on a ladder below the window, lighting the blazing bundles and tossing them through.

In a few minutes the earthen floor of the cell was thick with blazing rags. The end of a hose coiled like a black snake, through the window. Liquid dribbled down the wall, thickened into a steady stream. For a moment, as the puzzled Bill watched, he thought it was water. The liquid pooled on the floor, crept out in a steadily widening circle. The edge touched a fireball—and the entire cell exploded into roaring flame.

Pressed into a corner, clothing scorched, shielding his face from the searing heat with his Stetson, Bill heard a mocking voice outside the window, "How d'yuh fancy yore own medicine, yuh rat?" The inferno of flame was fast growing. It was plain to the gasping prisoner that he would soon be roasted alive. Bent low, he charged across the burning oil, darted over the passageway and plunged into the cell where Red watched with somber eyes.

In dreary silence, the two eyed the fire-filled cell and the stream of oil seeping from the hose high on the wall. Waves of heat beat against them, increasing in intensity as the pool lapped outward.

"Kid," said Red softly, "I guess this is whar we check out." His features creased as he nodded at the curling flames. "They shore give us a taste of what's ahaid when we sack our saddles."

"Le's go out shootin' and git it over!" urged Bill hoarsely.

"We'd never git through thet doorway, kid. Nope, we'll stick till our hides blister. Them Boxed T boys is my ace in the hole."

Slowly roasting, the pair crouched in a corner of the cell, as far from the flames as possible. Bill squinted at the slow-spreading puddle of liquid fire and speculated how many more minutes would pass before it drove them out through the doorway of death.

"Lissen, kid!" croaked Red.

The younger man strained his ears. Above the steady roar of the flames he thought he could hear distant yelling.

"They're acomin'!" The gunman's husky whisper was triumphant. "Mighty nigh time, I'm most fried tuh a crisp."

The yelling was plain now, interspersed with the boom of forty-fives.

"Le's go, kid! I ain't got much wool, but what there is is most singed off." Red grabbed his shotgun, dropped it with a fervent curse as the hot metal bit his fingers, and jumped for the doorway. Bill pressed after him.

As they leapt through quivering sheets of flame, Bill heard a renewed burst of gunfire and braced himself for the impact of lead. But no more bullets snicked into the firelit jail.

Clear of the flames, the pair spurted into the welcome cloak of darkness, dodging and twisting. Massed riders pounded past.

"Hey, Fiddlefoot!" yelled Bill.

The leader circled and brought his snorting pony to a standstill, a slightly built rider tailing him. "Jehoshaphat!" he ejaculated, in wonderment. "You alive! We figgered yuh was scorched to a cinder."

Bill looked back at the jail. The interior was a cauldron of restless flame, curling upward. It seemed impossible that they could have been trapped in that furnace so long, and live.

"Another five minutes and we'd have been steaks—well done," commented Red dryly.

The slightly built rider pulled up to Bill. Coppery hair glinted in the light of the blazing oil. His pulse jumped inexplicably as he recognized Tess Goodmer, clad in the plaid shirt and denims of a puncher.

"Hello, Mister Two-guns!" she bantered. "Don't look in a mirror or you'll die of shock."

Bill grinned crookedly. "It was mighty nice of yuh tuh bring the boys. These lunkheads around town got me all wrong. I was sidin' yore brother."

She nodded. "I know—the preacher told me. It's all an awful mess and it's been an awful day, for everyone."

"How's Jack makin' out?"

The girl's face clouded. "As well as we can hope, with a bullet through his lungs."

"I'll get Gleeko!" he promised tautly.

Impulsively, she reached down and placed her hand upon his shoulder. "Take care of yourself—Bill," she said quietly. There was an unwonted tenderness in her vibrant voice. Before he could reply, she heeled her pony and cantered away.

Fiddlefoot slung his long length out of the saddle. "Wal, it's all over now," he rumbled. "Painted Rock won't fergit this day in a hurry. And as f'r you, Bill, I never come acrost a jasper who could tangle with so much trouble so doggoned fast."

"Tangle!" repeated the young rider ruefully. "Hell, I don't have tuh tangle with it, it jest rushes at me, red-eyed, like a longhorn on the prod."

The Boxed T contingent, completing its circuit of the jail, jingled up. Few shots had been exchanged. The mob had melted into the night at the thundering approach of the rescue party.

"All the saloons go up in smoke?" inquired a puncher.

"The Highway to Hell's doin' business," volunteered another, "and I'm orful dry."

"Me, I'm so doggoned parched I caint spit," threw in Red. "Le's licker!"

The riders moved off toward the blackened remnants of the town, while the two scorched men followed afoot, Fiddlefoot leading his pony beside them.

Bitterness against Gleeko and his gang swept over Bill when they reached Main Street. The moon rode high, silvering the scene of destruction. Everything east of the broad street had escaped the conflagration. On the west side, however, nothing remained but smouldering heaps of cinders and charred timbers, out of which rock-and-adobe chimneys jutted up like dreary monuments. The rock-fronted bulk of the square-set bank stood intact, sooted and windows broken. The air was tainted with the dank odor of destruction.

Ghostly in the wan light, townsfolk wandered restlessly around the scanty remnants they had salvaged—iron bedsteads, tables, chairs—heaped in ragged piles down the street. No wonder, thought Bill, that they were in a lynching mood.

When he glimpsed his features in the back-bar mirror of the saloon, he gaped at the stranger who stared back with bloodshot eyes. His eyebrows had been singed off and his face was streaked with sooty smoke. A filthy bandage, scorched at the edges, circled his head and his clothes were in no better case.

He downed his drink, turned to Red, "My dun around?"

"In the livery, fed and watered."

"Guess I'll look him over." Pulling away from the bar, lined with exultant Boxed T riders, he stepped out into the street. Here he paused, soberly eying the scene of charred desolation, then walked rapidly in the direction of the livery barn. He had a double-barreled job—recover the loot stolen from the Grass Valley Bank and repay Gleeko for his treachery.

It was night again when a begrimed rider eased his gaunted pony through the bear grass and cactus that fringed El Infierno. The renegade roost, emptied of its birds of prey, slept. No light broke the drabness of the cluttered adobes until the lone horseman neared the frame building that housed the cantina. From the windows of the cantina, broad shafts of yellow lamplight patched the hoof-packed wagon road.

Bill checked the dun in the shadows, stepped down and ground-hitched the pony. He bent to unstrap his spurs. A wave of vertigo enveloped him. He overbalanced and pitched forward on his face. Fighting the sudden weakness, he struggled to his feet, clung to the saddle horn for support. His limbs were leaded by a cloying inertia and his entire body seemed drained of vitality. The bullet crease across his forehead felt as though it had been fresh branded with a hot iron. By sheer effort of will, he forced his stiff legs to function and wobbled stubbornly toward the cantina. The spurs were forgotten.

Two ponies stood, droop-hipped, at the rail outside. Bill glanced through the window, but he could only see one man, seated at a table, facing the doorway. It was Gleeko. A bottle and two glasses were set before him. Behind the plank bar, the fat Mexican, head cushioned upon his triple chins, dozed peacefully in an armchair.

At the jingle of spur chains, the barkeep awoke and gazed incuriously at the doorway. Bill swept aside the dust-laden curtains and stepped into the lamplight, a gun in his right hand.

The portly Mexican gasped, but Gleeko's features changed not one whit as he gazed into the muzzle.

"Howdy!" croaked Bill and grabbed at the curtains for support—Gleeko, the barkeep, the cantina, commenced to whirl in a dizzy fandango.

"Wal, ef it ain't the boss!" rasped the bank bandit. "Yuh look kinda tuckered out, pard. Rathole a drink!"

"Not with a dirty double-crosser," flung back Bill. His surroundings stopped their giddy whirl, he slithered crabwise to the bar, still holding his gun on Gleeko.

"Gimme a slug!" he grunted.

"*Si,* señor!" The fat man heaved eagerly out of his armchair, his bulk quivering. He reached down a bottle.

Narrowly watching Gleeko—or were there three Gleekos? The whole room was wavering uncertainly—the exhausted rider pulled the cork with his teeth, tilted the bottle and almost choked when the fiery liquor hit his dry throat. New life seemed to course through his veins and his vision steadied, but the support of the solid bar was still welcome.

The sour-faced bandit said nothing more, just sat, tensed and alert, watching the gun.

"Yuh know what I come f'r?" Bill's voice was stronger now.

"Shore, a cut. Wal, it's yores!"

"Cut, hell! I want it all—every damned dollar. Where yuh got it cached?"

Gleeko's thin face crinkled into what he intended to be a friendly grin. "Now quit funnin'," he soothed. "They's plenty f'r a divvy."

"I ain't askin' agen—Where is it? And keep them paws on the table!"

The bandit's thin fingers played a nervous tattoo on the stained table top. He threw a hasty, hopeful glance toward the curtained doorway, swallowed. "Cached outside of Painted Rock," he replied glibly.

Propped against the bar, not daring to stand erect for fear of another attack of vertigo, Bill sensed that the renegade was playing for time. Maybe his surviving pard was around.

"Yore a liar!" he snapped.

"Cross my heart, kid!"

Bill felt another spell of nausea approaching, Gleeko's form blurred. His grasp tightened up the heavy Colt that sagged in his fist. "Wal," he said thickly, thumbing the hammer, "yuh won't be around tuh collect." In an instant of clarity he saw Gleeko gesture to the barkeep, behind him, then the room vanished in a thunderclap and a shower of stars.

"Nice work, Tony!" approved Gleeko, scraping back his chair and rising without haste, as the gun dropped from Bill's nerveless fingers and his slack body slid slowly sideways, to sink in a muddled heap upon the packed earth floor.

CHAPTER SEVENTEEN

PUDGY FINGERS STILL CLENCHED around the neck of the bottle he had used as club, the barkeep bobbled around to set it on a shelf. Gleeko nudged Bill's form with a boot toe, to satisfy himself that the scorpion had lost its sting.

So it was that neither saw the smoke-blackened, hairless features of Red, as the saturnine gunman slipped silently through the curtained doorway. Both men jerked to startled attention at sound of his husky purr, "So yuh trumped the boss's ace! Wal, gents, I reckon I'll take the trick."

Tony, the fat barkeep, stood quivering like a mass of jelly, mouth agape. Slowly, his plump arms arose. But Red was watching Gleeko. The sour-faced bandit stood taut as a coiled watch spring, desperate hope in eyes that were focused past Red—on the curtained doorway.

For a second, two seconds, tight silence held the cantina.

Somewhere, outside, a spur chain clicked faintly. Red's eyes flicked toward the window. In a flash, the barkeep's right hand speared at the back of his neck. Came up with a slim blade. A flick of the wrist, and, with a hiss, it sped like a silver arrow across the room.

Red's gun blared as the sliver of steel bedded in his chest. A shriek tore from the barkeep's thick throat. He half twisted before the impact of a slug. The shriek died on his lips when Red, blood spreading fast over his shirt, threw down again and a bullet smashed squarely between the knifer's fat-bedded eyes. But Gleeko was in action. He flung sideways, throwing lead. At the same instant, Red whirled at a hammer click behind him. Outside, shrouded by darkness, Gleeko's pard fired through the curtains and Red's blood drained through another hole in his chest. He crashed, dropped his gun, snatched at his left-hand iron. Gleeko's gun thundered and the hard-stricken Red, game as a fighting cock, was hammered down. Life rapidly draining away, he levered head and shoulders from the floor, emptied his remaining gun through the doorway with a stuttering roar. Something akin to a grin twisted his pain-etched features as he heard the thud of a falling body, then the threshing of a mortally wounded man outside. Another slug from the crouching Gleeko shook his body. The smoking gun dropped from his fast-weakening grasp. A spasm of pain twisted his lined features. With a sigh his head dropped. Gleeko, thumbing the hammer, blinked through the powder fumes. The silence of death hung heavy on the smoke-filled room.

Gleeko, with a thin smile, straightened, plugged out his empties, reloaded. Loaded gun in his fist, he stepped to the side of Red's slack body, kicked the bloodied remains viciously, took a final glance around and holstered his iron. Then he hit for the door.

Bill drifted back to reality with the bite of burnt powder upon his nostrils. Befuddled, he blinked at the ceiling, black with flies. Recollection returned—Gleeko, the barkeep, the crash. He groaned, fingered a swelling on the back of his head. That was a bonehead play, he considered wryly, overlooking the barkeep. It it hadn't been for the thick bandage, the greaser would have cracked his skull, maybe beefed him.

A pony whinnied outside. Bill swayed to his feet, grasped the back of a chair and peered around. His bewildered eyes dwelt upon a body by the doorway. A jaunty red feather stuck in the band of a shabby Stetson that lay near by stirred memories in his mazed mind. Vainly, as he stared in perplexity, he strove to clarify his thoughts. A red feather? Red! But Red was in Painted

Rock! Rolling like a drunken man, Bill moved to the bar, leaned across it. The barkeep's stiffening form sprawled amid a litter of corks and cigarette butts. Weaving across the floor, Bill teetered above Red. The gunman's eyelids flicked up. The tight muscles of his lean face had relaxed and Bill's uncomprehending eyes looked down upon the seamed features of an old, weary man.

"So long, feller!"

At the husky whisper, Bill dropped to his knees beside the dying gunman. "How come yuh here?"

"Dogged yuh—figgered yuh'd hit fer—El Infierno." Red's voice gurgled away. Scarlet froth bubbled upon his lips. He swallowed, his lips moved again. Bill bent low to catch a feeble whisper, "Git Gleeko!" Then Red's head lolled sideways, the reflection of the hanging lamp overhead dull in his sightless eyes.

Gleeko! The gold! Like a knife thrust, memory of his mission stabbed into Bill's dulled mind. But where was Gleeko?

Upon uncertain feet he stumbled past the dirty curtains that draped the doorway, tripped over a prone form, heard a quick curse from a man swinging into the saddle at the hitch rail. A bulging gunny sack was tied behind the cantle.

The calico side-stepped nervously as Bill advanced upon uncertain legs. Gleeko steadied the animal with a quick jerk. His gun, still hot, leapt out of leather. "Gordamn yuh, I figgered yuh daid," he grated. The hammer clicked back.

Of their own volition, Bill's hands streaked for his forty-four's. Long, dreary years of incessant gun drill were paying their dividends. Like an automaton, incapable of clear thought, the stocky rider had spewed bullets at a piñon stump. This time the pinon stump was Gleeko.

A body slid heavily out of the saddle, spilled with a thud at the skittery calico's forefeet. Bill carefully bent down and squeezed beneath the rail. His head began to whirl again. The calico side-stepped nervously when he grabbed the horn to steady his faltering feet. He spoke soothingly to the animal, fingered the gunny sack, felt the unyielding bulges beneath the taut rawhide lashings and knew them to cover pouched gold. Without success he picked at the knots in the rawhide rope, fumbled fruitlessly in his pants pockets for a jackknife, then solved the problem—tonight everything seemed to be a problem—by leading the calico to the spot where he had left his pony in the shadows.

The dun still stood where he had dropped the reins. He hauled himself laboriously into the saddle, knotted the calico's reins around the horn and headed northward out of the sleeping settlement. Curious, he thought hazily, that the gunfire had brought no one around. Maybe there was so much shooting in El Infierno that another fracas meant nothing, or maybe the greasers had sense enough to stick inside their adobes when renegades went on the rampage. But the night had eyes.

In after years, Bill Carson could never clearly recall the details of his journey south to El Infierno and recovery of the Grass Valley Bank loot. The episode seemed as faint and elusive as a fading dream. He did remember stumbling out of the cantina with its dead, loosing lead at a shadowy form—or was it a piñon stump? Then, for countless aeons, riding—riding—riding.

The long night ride across the desert held more delirium than reality for the injured rider. Hour after hour the dun jogged steadily through sage and cactus, the calico trailing. Reins slack and stiffening fingers locked on the horn, Bill drooped lower and lower across his mount's withers. For the most part he dozed, in semicoma. At times he would awaken in delirium, flng high-pitched taunts at the ghostly ocatillos, whose spidery branches seemed to grope toward him; curse the sharp-barbed cholla that thrust its needles into his legs.

Overhead, a segment of moon floated in serene quiet among legions of flaming stars. Endlessly, the two ponies plodded across the barren waste. Bill, now deep sunk in stupor, wobbled like a stuffed dummy in rhythm with the dun's gait.

More than one rider, lost in the desert, whose only hope for survival lay in locating an elusive water hole, has found it by giving his pony its head. Animal instinct triumphs where human reasoning fails. Thus it was that when dawn plucked at the stars with pallid fingers, the vaquero bunched beneath his tilma on the ridge above Rocky Spring shouted a hoarse warning to the sleeping camp below. The cocoons around the cold ashes of a fire stirred sluggishly. Pancho Hernandez, spruce and alert even when rudely awakened in the half dark, was briskly mounting the slope before his followers had struggled out of their blankets.

"What is it, Enrique?" he inquired in Spanish, as he gained the summit of the ridge.

"A stranger, patron, with two horses. See! He rides in from the desert." Following the direction of the vaquero's pointing finger, Pancho focused a dun, footsore and gaunted, moving slowly through the patched mesquite, carrying the body of a man. Beside it, lagged a calico, lamed.

"Strange," murmured the Mexican, "strange!" He turned to the lookout. "You have done well, Enrique, you have eyes like the eagle. Pancho Hernandez does not forget." With this, he dropped down the bouldery slope. The vaqueros were astir now. A fire spluttered into life. Men rounded up their hobbled mounts.

Pancho stood by the spring and watched the two dust-mantled ponies head into the ravine. He stepped forward, checked the dun.

"By the Blessed Virgin, it is the Señor Carson!" he murmured, at sight of the unconscious rider's unshaven, heat-seared features. "Why does he ride from the south—alone?" The Mexican called sharply over his shoulder. Two vaqueros hurried forward, lifted the slack form from the saddle and laid it in the chaparral. "Give him water—only a little water," directed Pancho, who was severing the lashings of the gunny sack. It thudded heavily to the ground. Eagerly now, the Mexican cut the thong that bound the mouth of the sack, dipped inside and came out with a small leather pouch. When he opened it, yellow gold coin glinted richly in the growing light. A smile of understanding played upon Pancho's dark face.

The bright beams of the rising sun, streaming through a tracery of green above his head, brought Bill back, blinking, to consciousness. Except for a dull ache at the back of his head and a stiffness in his joints, nothing seemed amiss. For the span of several minutes he closed his eyes again, content to relax in dreamy ease. Memory nudged him—El Infierno, the dead men, Gleeko's pony, the loot. Fully awake now, he sat up. Not a dozen paces distant, vaqueros were gathered around a fire, eating. Hastily, Bill reached for his gun—but he had none. A well-remembered voice, suave and mocking, floated from the camp-fire, "You are feeling well again, I trust, Señor Carson?"

Stiffly, Bill gained his feet, moved out of the chaparral. His dun and the calico, gear stripped off, were feeding quietly beyond the pool. Pancho, a bulging gunny sack beside him, lounged against his saddle, sipping coffee.

"Ain't this Rocky Spring? How in hell did I git tuh be here?" demanded Bill, staring at the dark-featured vaqueros.

"The ways of El Dios are strange, señor. He breengs the wicked to judgment, and the good, such as I, Pancho Hernandez, receive their just reward."

"Thet's my gunny sack, yuh doggoned horsethief!"

"Let us rather say, señor," returned Pancho smoothly, "that the gunny sack ees yours, but the gold eet contains ees the property of the bank at Painted Rock. Yes?"

"Mebbe so, but I'm packin' it back tuh the bank."

"You are so funnee, señor," smiled the Mexican. "I should hang you, for you are wan beeg thief, but perhaps eet ees better that I let the sheriff do eet. I, Pancho Hernandez, weel return the stolen gold to the so happy citizens of Painted Rock, and I weel return you—to the cell where you belong."

Bill's eyes sparked anger as he grasped the implications of the smooth Mexican's words.

"Say, get this, Pancho—" he began, his voice brittle, but the other checked him with upraised hand. "Leesen, señor! Your ban-ditoes robbed the bank and fired the town, as they fired my rancho. Two escaped with the gold, but you were caught. Your renegades rescued you from the carcel. You, what you say, spleet the breeze out of town. Poof! You are gone. Then, a miracle! I am camped at Rocky Spring, and behold you are delivered into my hands, weeth the loot. Verily, the Saints are kind! Eet ees plain you keeled your compañeros. You double-cross even them for gold. But you are lost in the desert, your senses leave you, your pony drifts to water. Yes, the Saints are just, *muy* just!"

"Lissen!" grated Bill, "I trailed Gleeko tuh El Infierno and grabbed thet loot. Was headin' f'r Painted Rock when I passed out. Thet dinero belongs tuh the bank."

"Eet weel be returned, as I have said," smiled Pancho, "and as I also have said, you weel be returned, too."

It was noon when the procession wound down the devastated main street of Painted Rock. First came Pancho. At the tail of his pony, wrists lashed to the horn, rode Bill. Behind them trailed a string of vaqueros.

Pancho was in fine fettle. First he made a speech to the crowd that gathered around outside the bank. Followed a triumphal march into the bank, the heavy gunny sack balanced upon his shoulder. Meanwhile, Bill, surrounded by derisive, hostile-eyed townsmen, gloomed in bitterness of spirit. To overflow his cup of woe, he glimpsed Tess Goodmer on the outskirts of the crowd.

Again he was lodged in the adobe jail, now blackened and burnt out. The cell was destitute of bunk or blankets. Unshaven, grimy and forlorn, he hunkered against the wall and awaited his fate.

Through town, the good news spread fast—Pancho Hernandez had recaptured the leader of the renegade gang and recovered the gold looted from the bank.

The second day, Bill had a visitor, Fiddlefoot. The ancient, tobacco-chewing guard stationed himself at one end of the passageway, while another old-timer, toting a shotgun, stood by the door. They were taking no chances of another break.

"Ef yuh ain't the darndest young hellion f'r gittin' inter jack pots!" rumbled the bean pole. "Why in the name of creation did yuh hev tuh ride plumb inter Pancho's camp, packin' a chunk of holdup gold?"

Bill told of his ride to El Infierno, his knockout by the bartender and his ride across the desert to return the looted gold. "Reckon I passed out and then the dun packed me tuh Rocky Spring," he concluded. "My head was doin' handsprings after thet conk."

Fiddlefoot pondered. "Cain't ease yuh outa this joint agen. Sheriff's ridin' in on the Deever stage t'morrow. They's been too much hell around Grass Valley and the bank holdup forced his hand. This is a gosh-awful spot yore on, Bill."

"Would I have rode north, if I grabbed the gold, like Pancho claims? Heck, I woulda been safe across the Border!"

"Yuh got a good point there," agreed Fiddlefoot, "but there ain't a citizen around town who ain't itchin' tuh see yuh swing."

"Jack Goodmer still alive?"

"Was when I last heard."

"He can testify I sided him."

"It still 'pears mighty ugly tuh me," said Fleetfoot doubtfully.

"How's the range ruckus?"

"Kinda slowed up. Jim paid off yore renegades, sez thet if he can't whip the lousy sheepherders thet call theirselves cowmen with his own crew he'll throw in his hand. The old moseyhorn's on his feet agen and exceedin' rambunctious. Wal, I gotta drift." And the tall rider left Bill to his thoughts.

Hours dragged for the man caged in the stinking adobe. The longer he considered his situation, the more hopeless it seemed. The twist of fate that threw him into Pancho's hands had set the seal of guilt squarely upon him. The least he could expect was a long penitentiary term—for a crime he did not commit. And the cause of all his trouble was that suave devil Pancho Hernandez.

Bitter resentment mounted as he restlessly paced the cell. He'd ridden a straight trail and it had brought him nothing but a prison cell. His paw was a renegade, he'd turn renegade, too. He should have done the job his paw had sent him to do. A stubborn determination seized him to break jail and get the Mexican. After he'd squared accounts with Pancho, he'd gun Jim Thompson. Then he'd hit for the Border. If he hadn't been soft-headed, he'd never have landed in this jack pot. Well, he thought savagely, he would not make the same mistake again.

Shortly after sundown, the jingle of the padlocked chain that secured a makeshift outer door announced the arrival of his supper. The tobacco-chewing old-timer shuffled in, carrying a laden tray. He set it on the floor outside the cell, passed the contents, one by one, between the bars.

Bill accepted mug and spoon lifelessly. Grumbling, the old-timer bent to slide the plate of beef and beans beneath the gate. The prisoner galvanzed into swift action. His right hand shot between the bars and clamped on the jailor's wrist. A jerk, and the surprised man sprawled awkwardly forward. Bill's left hand snatched the holstered gun, lifted it out of the holster, swung the barrel against the side of the guard's head. With a groan, the jailor collapsed. The prisoner stretched both arms through the bars, hauled the limp form close, fished the key to the cell door out of a pants pocket. In seconds he was standing out in the passageway, buckling on the jailor's gunbelt.

He dragged the other inside the cell and clanged the gate shut. Yell as loud as he might, the jail was set too far back on the flat for the unwilling prisoner to attract attention.

Thrilled by his new-found freedom and the bump of a gun against his leg, Bill strode to the outer door. Never, he vowed mentally, would he enter that jail again—alive.

CHAPTER EIGHTEEN

ON THE VERY THRESHOLD OF FREEDOM—at the door of the jail—Bill hesitated. Once outside, how would he make his getaway? It was a sure thing he could not leg it to Pancho's spread. His pony had probably been turned into the corral adjoining the livery barn. Odds were that Judd, the liveryman, would be working around and would yell blue murder if he attempted to toll the animal away. Besides, he needed saddle and bridle, and they would be inside the barn. Dammit, he just *had* to get hold of a mount—a rider afoot off Main Street would be as conspicuous as a saddled steer.

Loud gurgling from the cell behind him indicated that the jailor was recovering his senses. Throwing caution aside, Bill pushed open the door, stepped outside without apparent haste, slammed the makeshift door and clamped the padlock on the hasp. He tossed the ring of keys into a tangle of weeds.

Casually, he sauntered toward the rear of the marshal's office, a hundred paces distant. Pulse hammering, he gained the cover of the darkened alley that separated the lawman's shack from the Chink restaurant, adjoining. His pace quickened. He slid down the alley like a shadow. At its mouth, he checked, stuck out his head and swiftly scanned graying Main Street. The further side was a charred waste, littered with the burnt skeletons of homes. To his right, a scattering of ponies were tied outside The Highway to Hell, plain in the lamplight that slanted from the saloon windows and madly tantalizing to the fugitive. It was hopeless, he saw, to attempt to grab one, he would be in full view of the patrons inside. And there was not another pony tied within sight.

A muffled shouting issued from the jail. To the man crouching in the darkened alley it seemed thunderous in the evening quiet.

The muffled clip-clop of a pony's hooves pulled his head around again. A rider jogged leisurely upstreet. Bill shrank back into the shadows as the newcomer reined up at the hitch rail, almost within grasp. He swung to the ground, knotted his reins around the smooth rail, stepped across the plankwalk and flattened his nose against the window of the town marshal's office. Apparently, the shack was empty, for, whistling blithely, the rider jingled off past the store front, pushed through the batwings into The Highway to Hell.

Bill eyed the pony, a clean-limbed claybank, built for speed. He stepped sideways and surveyed the brand. It was one of the Limey's horses, from the Frying Pan. They claimed the Englishman raised the best in the Valley. Without further hesitation, Bill crossed the plankwalk, loosed the knotted reins and stepped into the saddle. The claybank crowhopped at the feel of a strange hand on the bit. Ears attuned for a yell of alarm, Bill eased the animal around, thankful for the dust fog churned up by the dancing hooves. With a final protesting snort, the claybank settled down to a steady trot. In a few minutes, the exulting Bill was clear of Main Street. He shook the pony into a lope, followed the wagon road that snaked down to the ford. Behind him, the town was still silent. He chuckled with relief. Lady Luck was siding him at last. He was a horsethief now, as well as an accused bank robber, he mused whimsically. Well, they could only hang a man once if he held up every bank and stole every doggoned horse in the West.

Dawn found the fugitive belly-flat on a mesquite bench on the fringe of the Black Hills. He felt the warmth of the rising sun on his back as he gazed down at a cluster of buildings, huddled in the narrow valley below. The terrain was not unfamiliar. Once before he had ridden up that valley at the head of his renegades and made a hash of Pancho Hernandez's home spread. The scars were still plain—blackened duins of what once had been barn and ranch house. But the water tank had been repaired and the clutter of weather-stained adobes in which Pancho's vaqueros and their families lived were untouched.

As the sun rose, he saw the ranch stir to greet the new day. Smoke curled from cooking fires into the clear air; sombreroed vaqueros stretched and yawned around the adobes; a yelling youth hazed in the remuda.

A muttered exclamation left the watcher's lips as a lithe rider, scarlet sash vivid around his waist, stepped briskly into view. Coat shining, the silver buckles and conchas on its gear gleaming, a black was led out. With a wave of the hand toward the adobes, Pancho stepped lightly into the saddle and headed down valley.

On the bench high above, Bill hastily squirmed around and wormed back through the mesquite. Lady Luck was surely atoning for her past lapses. He had been racking his brains to devise a means of getting at Pancho and here his enemy had solved the problem pronto.

Out of sight of the vaqueros in the valley below, Bill jumped to his feet, spurted through the brush, checked at a tangle of witch hopple and chokecherry. From its midst, he led out the claybank, vaulted into the saddle and pricked the animal into a gallop. Angling across the bench, he dropped down into a ravine, spurred recklessly through the chaparral.

At the mouth of the ravine, a twisted oak, mossy with age, thrust out knotted branches. A few paces beyond, wheel ruts marked the trail from the P/H.

Bill tied the claybank behind a screen of rustling aspens, hefted a coiled rope and took up position behind the thick trunk of the oak. With a tight smile of anticipation, he examined the jailor's six gun, pressed the release key and let the cylinder drop into his palm. Carefully he checked the loads. Satisfied, he replaced the cylinder in the frame and slid the pin home. This was one time he was determined to leave nothing to chance.

The faint tinkle of conchas made music in his ears. That greaser, he thought in silent mockery, made as much music as a brass band. Ears alert, he waited, judging his time.

Hooves thudded softly. In high spirits, Pancho hummed a gay tune. It died abruptly as a grim, unshaven rider stepped out from behind the oak, six gun leveled.

The rattle of the black's bit chains, as it tossed its head, impatient of the quick curb, was loud in the taut silence. Pancho spoke first:

"Greetings, señor! Ees there no carcel built that weel hold you?"

"Not when I want tuh get you!"

"Have you not keeled enough?"

"Nope, I'm all set to beef one more chili-eater." There was a flat finality in Bill's voice that tightened the Mexicans lips beneath the smudge of mustache. Then his white teeth gleamed in a quick laugh. "But, Señor Carson, are you not a gunman, who keels for pay? You weel get no pay if you keel me—you weel get the rope around your neck. Even now I ride to meet the good sheriff."

"Yuh'll never meet the sheriff, greaser!" said Bill stonily. "Yore gonna hang—'member when yuh was all set tuh hang me? 'Member the bunch of Boxed T jaspers yuh butchered at the ford? Wal, this is where yuh pay. Git down!"

Fear dawned in Pancho's sharp eyes, but his voice was still steady. "Señor, geeve me—what you call eet—an even break. If I die, let eet be weeth a gun in my hand, not by a rope, like a ladron."

"Step down!" snapped the grim gunman.

Pancho opened his mouth to speak again, read the message of death in the flinty blue eyes behind the leveled Colt, swung slowly out of his saddle. Desperately, he tried a final appeal, "My life eet ees worth a thousand dollars—gold, señor."

"A million wouldn't buy it!" Bill assured him harshly.

The Mexican shrugged. Whatever Pancho was, he sure wasn't yellow, conceded the Boxed T rider, with unwilling admiration.

"May I smoke—wan cigarillo?"

"And sneak a draw—nope!"

Bill stooped, eyes never leaving Pancho, debonair even in the face of death. He groped for the coiled rope with his free hand, straightened with a jerk as the quick tattoo of a pony's hooves, approaching at a fast gallop from the direction of the ranch, was plain. He stepped back hastily behind the tree trunk, still covering Pancho, only his gun and half his face visible. "Hold it!" he cautioned coldly.

Both waited—Bill Carson with angry impatience. Looked like he'd have to plug Pancho, when he was all set to hang the lobo: the Mexican nursing a forlorn hope that this might mean a reprieve from death.

A chestnut gelding streaked around a bend in the trail, swept toward them, reared high when it was jerked to a sudden stop.

"Why, Pancho—what's wrong?"

Concealed by the tree trunk, Bill almost dropped his gun in startled surprise. A girl rode the gelding. A girl whose fluffy hair, upon which a stiff-brimmed Stetson had been hastily jammed, made an aura of spun gold in the sunlight. It was Mildred Thompson—and she was living on Pancho's ranch! Not content with knifing Jim Thompson, the Mexican had robbed him of his daughter. Bleak-eyed, Bill stepped into view.

Pancho smiled, as the other surveyed him—a wan ghost of a smile. "Eet ees best that you should return to the rancho, *querida mia*." But Mildred Thompson was staring blankly at the trail-stained interloper with the leveled gun.

"Bill Carson!" she breathed. "What are you doing here?"

"Payin' off a debt, ma'am," returned Bill shortly. "Yuh best vamoose, back to the Boxed T."

"Take your gun off my husband!" she cried imperiously. "And ride for the Border before a posse gets on your trail."

"You two hitched?" Bill flung the incredulous question at Pancho. The Mexican glanced fondly at the indignant girl. "*Si*, señor!"

"Wal, ef I don't string yuh up, Thompson shore will."

"I hate Jim Thompson!" broke in the girl passionately.

Bill ignored her. "Yuh shore earned the rope, greaser. First, yuh knife Thompson. Then, when he's on his back, yuh grab his gal."

He stepped close, until his gun barrel nudged the scarlet sash, reached with his left hand, unbuckled Pancho's gunbelt. As the gunbelt dropped, he scaled the Mexican's huge sombrero into the brush. Then, with a quick motion, flicked a loop over the Mexican's head.

The manila sang through the honda as he jerked the loop tight. Without warning, the girl flew at him, clawing like a wildcat. Gun in one hand, rope in the other, Bill was at a disadvantage. He retreated backward, fending off the golden-haired fury with his elbows, dragging the helpless Pancho with him.

Beneath the tree, he sent his feminine assailant reeling with a forcible push, took advantage of the brief respite to toss the rope over a low-hanging branch. He caught the loose coil as it fell. A quick tug, and Pancho, half strangled, was hauled up to tiptoe beneath the branch. Bill dropped his gun into the holster, the rope taut in his left fist. He had one hand free to handle Thompson's crazy daughter now.

The girl regained balance and came at him again. But now her hands were extended and there were tears in her eyes. "Carson," sh panted, "you can't do this awful thing. Pancho's my husband. Do you hear? My husband!"

"The rattlesnake knifed Thompson." Bill put his weight on the rope, cold eyes watching the helpless Mexican's features blacken and tongue protrude as he tore at the strangling thong with both hands in frantic efforts to ease the choking constriction upon his windpipe. Bill thought of a certain night beside Lost River and the deep-cut blue weal around his own neck. The Mex didn't seem to savor his own medicine.

"Wait!" screamed the girl. "I knifed Jim Thompson, and I'm not his daughter."

"More windies!" grunted Bill, but he eased the rope. Pancho Hernandez didn't deserve a quick death.

"Listen, for God's sake, listen!" Sobbing, she pawed at him. "Twelve years ago, when I was six, Thompson's riders burned our shack and killed my parents. They were nesters. I hid in the wagon. They found me and carried me back to the ranch. Thompson adopted me. He was kind, but I could never forget. I hated him then, I hate him now!"

"Cut it short!" grunted Bill, twitching the rope.

"I met Pancho at school. We rode together, roamed the hills, until Thompson heard about it. He forbade me to see Pancho again, said he wouldn't have his girl, his girl, mind you!"—her voice hose high in mounting hysteria—"get friendly with a greaser. But I always loved Pancho and always will."

"The knifin'?" Bill was less certain now.

"Jim Thompson was ruthless. He held by force all the choice range in the Valley. He knew Pancho needed more grass, and the other ranchers were restive, so he hired gunmen, like you. I could see, only too plainly, that it would all lead to fighting and killing and misery. If one man were dead—Thompson—there would be nothing to fight about. He was the cause of all the trouble. He has no heirs, no relatives. The night you rode in, I tried hard to kill him. I wish I had! Now hang me!" Defiant, she faced Bill with streaming eyes.

He frowned at her in perplexity. "Is that story straight?" he threw at the Mexican.

"*Si,* señor!" vouched Pancho hoarsely. He was stretched erect, both hands locked on the rope overhead, striving to ease the noose to the utmost.

Bill rasped his stubbled chin. This unexpected twist tangled him. Who was he to sit in judgment upon Mildred Thompson, or Hernandez, or whatever her danged name was. Hadn't he ridden into Grass Valley to kill Thompson himself? Impulsively, he slackened the rope. "Skeedaddle!" he told the Mexican curtly. His lips curled with cold humor, "Now we both got a rope burn across our gizzards."

Common sense urged the escaped prisoner to head for the Border. But he had a chore to handle before he left Grass Valley, a chore he had shirked too long, he told himself stonily, as the claybank plowed through a sea of grass toward the Boxed T. His paw had spent years readying him for just one job. Crawler was a helpless cripple, he had to trust his son—and his son had shilly-shallied around, done nothing but tangle his spurs. This time, determined Bill, he'd see it through. A hombre who could butcher helpless nesters and steal a scared little girl would not be slow to throw a slug into a man's backbone. Yet he'd been loco enough to side Thompson—the man he rightly should have killed the first time they met. Yes, pondered the rider, his brains had sure bogged down.

Hunkered around the yard, the Boxed T crew were digesting supper when Bill rode in. They eyed the fugitive's disheveled figure with poker faces that hid a lively curiosity. Everyone in the Valley knew he had been recaptured with the bank loot. It was plain that he had broken jail and it was their duty as citizens to turn him over to the law. But the Boxed T bunch had both a healthy respect for his gun and a liking for the chunky rider who had led them against the hostile spreads. It the law wanted him, let the law corral him! They were strictly neutral, even though he straddled a prime peace of horseflesh carrying the Frying Pan brand.

Fiddlefoot was in the bunkhouse, as was evidenced by the plaintive plink-plonk of his beloved banjo. Bill watered his mount, tied it loosely by the trough. He might need to make a quick getaway.

A rapt expression upon his bony features, Fiddlefoot sat alone on the floor below his bunk, deep-sunken eyes fixed on the ceiling as he strummed mournfully with his left hand.

"Thompson around?" demanded Bill abruptly, striding through the doorway.

The lanky rider quit in the middle of a chord. "Heck!" he rumbled, "I shore thought it was a haunt. Ain't yuh in the hoose gow?"

"I done busted out."

Fiddlefoot groaned. "Bank robbery, arson, unlawful woundin', breakin' jail. Hell, Bill yuh'll draw most a hundred years, mebbe two."

"Yuh fergot hoss stealin'—they hang men f'r thet in Texas."

"Likewise in Arizona. What in hell got inter yuh?"

"Yuh ain't said ef Thompson's around."

"Nope, he rode tuh town. Sheriff Tighman done come in on the stage, snortin' fire and brimstone. He called all the Grass Valley cowmen tuh Painted Rock f'r a powwow. I got ten cart wheels thet sez there ain't no more range war from now on." The tall rider set the battered banjo tenderly on the table, jerked the makin's from his shirt pocket. "How come yuh left the hoosegow so danged sudden?"

"Tuh git Pancho." Bill told of his trip to the P/H and the startling story of Mildred Thompson.

Fiddlefoot showed no surprise. "She give yuh the straight. The gal's been sweet on Pancho all through, but Jim Thompson hated the greaser's guts. I figgered a Mex never knifed Jim. He woulda made a shore job of it. I guess she couldn't throw good.

So she never fergot her folks!" He paused, meditatively expelled smoke through his nose. "Wal, who'd hev placed thet gal f'r a killer. Yuh never kin figger a woman, Bill! She beat it three—four days back—left a note. It didn't faze Jim none. He jest folded it inter a spill and lit a cigarette with it. I gotta hunch he was wise tuh the gal—right along. And I ain't blamin' him f'r rubbin' out her folks."

"I'd call it plain murder," said Bill baldly.

The tall man eyed him with calm speculation. When he replied, there was a rasp of hostiity in his deep voice, "W·hat would you know about it? Them was tough times. Raidin' 'Paches and thievin' nesters. Cowmen hunted the Injuns like rattlesnakes and the nesters like wolves—they was a worse pest than wolves, butcherin' cows, rustlin' calves, fencin' water, startin' fires. Hell, a man had tuh keep his range clean tuh survive."

A pony's hooves clattered in the yard. Fiddlefoot reached for his banjo, "Wal, ef yuh crave tuh see the old moseyhorn, his broomtail jest drifted in."

Bill stamped out his smoke, rose. The tall man eyed him curiously as he mechanically hefted the gun at his side and eased it into the holster. Slowly, he moved toward the door.

"So long!" rumbled Fiddlefoot, striking a note.

"Adios!" returned Bill absently.

CHAPTER NINETEEN

EVERY BRAND IN THE VALLEY but one was burned into the coats of the ponies tied around the white frame bungalow that was the home of the Goodmers, in the shadow of the butte behind Painted Rock. And the slack-hipped ponies, lazily watching flies in the sunlight, were a heap more relaxed than their owners inside the house.

A brittle hostility pervaded the living room, where the cowmen gathered, an hostility plainly directed toward the square-set figure of Jim Thompson. Not that it fazed the owner of the Boxed T. In fact, something akin to amusement lurked in his flinty eyes. Back against the cold stove, he stood erect, craggy jaw outthrust, watching his hostile neighbors, as they fidgeted in various parts of the room. By the front window, heavy-set Chris Hansen moodily chewed a chaw of tobacco. Wiry Fred Taylor, ramrod of the Rocking T, and squat bald-headed Tom Clausen, owner of the big Circle S, jerked words at each other in low-voiced talk. Chaucer-Smyth, the Englishman, puffed a briar pipe and regarded everyone with an amiable smile from the depths of a well-padded rocker.

Pale, his face pinched with pain, Town Marshal Goodmer was propped up with pillows in an armchair. He gazed half humorously at the fleshy features, damp with perspiration, of a bulky man in dark coat and pants. A sheriff's badge was pinned to the big man's gray shirt. The unobservant might place him as a beefy, good-natured bull—overlooking the heavy jaw beneath the rolls of fat that layered the lawman's jowls and the disconcerting steadiness that lay in his shrewd eyes. Sheriff Sam Tighman had not been re-elected four times in succession without good reason.

The sheriff bit the tip off a thin black cigar and spat it irritably in the direction of the stove. "Ef this Pancho hombre don't drift in before thet clock hits the hour," he told the wounded marshal, with a touch of asperity, "I'll go git the hairpin and bring him in—handcuffed."

"Mebbe his hoss broke a leg, Sam," suggested Goodmer soothingly. "Yuh never kin tell."

"Mebbe he drowned crossing Lost River," grunted Tighman, "or mebbe the hombre growed too big f'r his boots, which is more likely."

At a sudden clatter of hooves outside, all eyes went to the front windows. A black, sweat daubed, was reined down to a sliding halt. Before the pebbles stopped splattering, a resplendent figure swung out of the high-pommeled saddle, swaggered toward the house.

"The Latin temperament," murmured Chaucer-Smyth, "spectacular and all that sort of thing."

"I set this meetin' f'r noon, Hernandez," barked the sheriff, as the ever-smiling Pancho strutted into the room.

"A thousand pardons, señor!" The Mexican indicated the dust-grayed bandage around his neck. "My pony, he spook—he bolt—a branch hook me by the throat, like a feesh—I am delayed—I am so sorree!"

Tighman cleared his throat and raised his voice, "Wal, I guess we're all here. I don't hev tuh tell you gents why I come down from the county seat. Yuh know I ain't in the habit of hornin' inter pussonal dogfights, but this Grass Valley ruckus ain't pussonal no longer. When yore gunhands burn down half the town, bust inter the bank, cripple the marshal, I got no choice but tuh take a hand."

"Whose gunhands?" demanded Clausen, glowering at the Boxed T boss.

"Thompson's, the same hawg who smoked me out," snapped Taylor. "Set the blame whar it belongs, Sheriff!"

Jim Thompson's jaw jutted, "Who started this fracas?"

"Who set hees guards on the so precious water?" inquired Pancho silkily. "And who theenks he ees keeng?"

"Button up!" snapped the sheriff. "I didn't swaller dust f'r six hours tuh lissen tuh yore whittle-whangin'."

"No man was ever convinced by argument," observed Chaucer-Smyth oracularly. "Count me on your side, Sheriff. Fighting is horribly inconvenient, particularly during the hot months."

"Quit dribblin'!" advised Tighman caustically. "Now lissen, you lobos! Yuh gotta quit and quit right here and now. Folks are sayin' there's no law in Grass Valley, and askin' why the hell did they elect a sheriff. I'm servin' notice on you, Jim Thompson, you, Hernandez and you other gents—quit! Ef any cowman crosses another's boundary line, or looses another slug, I'll be streakin' on his trail with a posse, and I swear I'll set the hombre behind bars. Ef a posse ain't strong enough tuh cut yore claws, dammit, they's the U.S. cavalry at Fort Apache. Is thet plain?"

"Perfectly, old top!" threw in Chaucer-Smyth. "Your English, though it lacks elegance, is both forceful and explicit."

"Bottle up, Limey! Anyone else got anythin' tuh stick in?" Tighman glanced expectantly around, a challenge in his narrow eyes.

"I, for one, am perfectly willing to shake hands and call it a day," came back the unabashed Chaucer-Smyth.

"How about you, Clausen—and you, Hernandez?"

The Circle S owner jerked his head in curt agreement. Pancho flashed his white teeth. "Why fight when we can leeve together like wan beeg happy family?" There was a touch of malice in the glance he directed at Thompson, but the old cowman either ignored or missed it.

"Taylor?" tallied the sheriff.

"I ain't buckin' the law."

"And you—Hansen?"

The Swede raised his heavy shoulders, "Jim Thompson never stomped on me."

Tighman dabbed his damp forehead with a red bandana, obviously relieved. "Wal, thet's that! We bury the hatchet. No range war never brought nothin' but grief. Yuh kin pay off them gun sharks, Thompson."

"They're done paid off—with a bonus." The old cowman turned toward the door. On the threshold, he paused, his head came around and his deep-set eyes challenged them, "And I kin hire 'em agen—pronto!"

The room emptied, save for Tighman and the wounded town marshal. The sheriff dropped into a chair. "No more sense than a pack of Siwashes," he grumbled. "Fifteen, twenty waddies beefed, two spreads smoked up, a town most wiped out. And what does it bring 'em? Nothin'! They rip out each other's guts f'r a fistful of range—and they's a million acres hereabouts. By jimminy, it most slipped my mind! I got tuh git out a warrant f'r thet Carson lobo."

Jack Goodmer's eyes clouded. "Yuh ain't got the rights on thet matter, Sam. He done busted jail agen. They's a posse of townsmen combin' the Black Hills f'r him right now. I wouldn't deputize the jugheads, but they rode notwithstandin'."

"I don't git yuh!" Tighman eyed the marshal, eyes probing.

"Carson's as innercent as a newborn calf."

"Hell's bells!" exploded the sheriff. "Didn't the maverick bust inter the bank, fire the town and git away with a stack of coin?"

"Nope!" came back Goodmer wearily. His weakness made talking an effort. "Lemme give yuh the low-down." He told of Bill's part in the bank raid.

"How come he was picked up with the loot?" asked Tighman doubtfully.

Tess, trim and efficient, bustled in, carrying a tray upon which were set a plate of homemade cookies, a bottle of bourbon and a glass. She set it down beside the sheriff.

"Your medicine!" she smiled.

Tighman's eyes brightened. He bit into a cooky, poured a stiff peg. "Ma'am, ef and when I git lead pisonin', I'll shore nominate you f'r nurse."

The girl dropped into a rocker. "Now, Mr. Tighman, I'm going to answer your last question. Jack needs rest, he's done too much talking. Bill Carson was a victim of circumstances. He hired gunmen to fight for the Boxed T. Some of them got out of hand and raided the bank. He raced to town, to warn Jack, but he was too late. He fought the gunmen at Jack's side. In the confusion, he was jailed. Jack was unconscious, so he couldn't set things right. Just as soon as Carson was released, he rode south—to recover the loot. I am convinced of that because we have a Mexican woman who cleans up around here. She has cousins in El Infierno. They told her that a man with blackened features rode in on a dun pony, and that the man was Bill Carson. There was gunfire in the cantina. The man came out, untied a pony with a heavy gunny sack lashed behind the cantle and led it north. They found four bodies around the cantina. Bill Carson fought them for the loot. He was wounded, lost consciousness in the desert and his pony headed for water. Pancho and his vaqueros were camped at the spring. That's how he was captured." She leaned forward in earnest appeal, gray eyes pleading, "Now, if he didn't intend to return the loot, why did he ride north? He was safe south of the Border."

Tighman munched the last of the cookies in silence; the bourbon gurgled as he tilted the bottle. The sheriff was feeling mighty spry—hadn't he stopped a range war singlehanded? That wouldn't hurt his prestige, and there was an election coming up. The cookies were good, too, and the whisky choice.

"Ma'am," he drawled, "it's a pleasure tuh meet a dandy cook, a good lawyer and a danged pritty gal, all in one. Yuh plumb got me hawg-tied with yore argyment—I guess we'll fergit thet warrant."

Tess's face flushed. "That's wonderful!" she breathed.

"Kinda sweet on the lobo?"

She crimsoned, jumped to her feet. "Why, Mr. Tighman, you do get the strangest ideas! Bill Carson is the most obstinate, the most aggravating—"

"Invite me tuh the weddin'," broke in the sheriff, chuckling. She fled to the kitchen.

Jim Thompson was watering his pony when Bill stepped out of the bunkhouse. Unsighted in the fading light, he watched the cowman hand the animal over to a puncher, who commenced to strip off the gear. Thompson walked toward the house, talking with two waddies.

At the house, the two riders turned away and the rancher stepped inside. Bill hurried across the yard.

The kitchen was empty when he pushed open the door. He crossed it quickly, hesitated in the corridor beyond. His ear caught the jingle of spur chains. He moved toward the sound, glimpsed the cowman alone in the spacious living room, unstrapping his spurs.

At sound of the interloper, Thompson glanced up. If he felt surprise at sight of Bill's scorched, unshaven features and tight-set lips, he showed none. He tossed his spurs to one side and sank into a rocker. "Step right in, son!" he called.

Bill slid through the doorway, stood tensed, face hard-set.

"Grab a seat and rest yore laigs," invited Thompson carelessly, "Yuh look like yore on the lam."

"I busted out of the hoosegow, yesterday." His visitor stood stockstill by the doorway.

"So I heard—yuh loot thet bank?"

"Nope!"

"Plenty figger yuh did."

"They figgered wrong!" Bill's voice was harsh with restrained emotion. Why did he have to spur himself so relentlessly to shoot this man? He had good cause, hadn't he? Didn't Thompson cripple his paw?

" 'Member why I rode into Grass Valley?"

The old cowman rolled a smoke with steady fingers. "Shore!"

"Wal, yore packin' a gun—draw it!"

Thompson touched his tongue to the cigarette paper, struck a match. " 'Pears yore everlastin' on the prod, son," he said mildly.

"Yuh wiggled out of a showdown once, Thompson—yuh ain't runnin' another sandy over me. Go f'r yore gun!" Bill's voice was strained; his fingers twitched at the butt of the gun holstered at his side.

"Set down, le's chew this over," urged the cowman, eying the taut-featured, nerve-frayed fugitive with more curiosity than fear.

"I'm through talkin'—yellerbelly!" Almost reluctantly, as though impelled by a power beyond his will. Bill jerked the gun. The hammer clicked back. He threw down on the rugged-faced man who sat unmoved in the rocker.

"I'm countin' five, Thompson." His voice was a husky whisper, almost inaudible. "I'm givin' yuh a break, thet's more than yuh give paw. Stand up and fight like a man, or yore shore enough cashin' in."

Slowly, he began to count, the sweat gathering in tiny beads upon his forehead, "One—two—three—"

CHAPTER TWENTY

"FOUR!" Sweat-bathed, Bill voiced the count. A sharp rap on the heavy outer door on the far side of the room jangled upon his raw nerves. He paused uncertainly.

Another rap and the mumble of voices and the jingle of impatient feet was plain outside.

"Ignoring the pointed gun, Thompson rose, crossed the room and squinted through one of the slit windows. " 'Pears like a posse tuh me," he commented laconically. "Yuh best beat it, son." There was no relief or triumph at the unexpected respite from what was apparently sure death in his dry tone.

Indecision racked the rider, keyed to kill. What was the old catamount's game? In seconds, Thompson could throw open the door, the posse would flood in and he would be a prisoner. Even a shout of alarm from the cowman would bring them at the run. But here was Thompson advising him to escape!

Baffled, he stood irresolutely, gun arm sagging.

"Skeedaddle!" barked the old cowman.

Reason whispered to Bill that now was the time to plug Thompson—now or never. Before the jostling men outside could sense the killing he would have time to dash through the kitchen, slip out of the rear door, mount the fast-stepping Frying Pan pony and make a clean getaway in the gathering darkness. Even as the thought struck him, he rejected it, and in a blinding flash of illumination knew that for some deep-seated, unfathomable reason he could not shoot Jim Thompson in cold blood.

With almost a gesture of relief he dropped the gun into leather, glanced quickly around. The rapping was violent now; the possemen were becoming restive. To his left the door of a darkened room stood invitingly open. He stepped through the doorway, found himself in a bedroom. Closing the door until it was scarcely ajar, he stood listening—and thanked the hunch that had deterred him from following the obvious pathway of escape, through the kitchen into the yard. As Thompson swung the front door wide open and admitted a press of armed men, others cascaded into the living room from the kitchen. It was evident that they had become impatient, or suspicious, and surrounded the ranch house.

"Wal, gents," questioned the old cowman, stonily, "how come yore in such an all-fired rush?"

"Bill Carson around?" inquired a sharp voice.

"Nope!"

Amid the rumble of voices and shuffle of spurred boots, the fugitive heard Fiddlefoot's deep rumble, "What's the ruckus, gents?"

"Carson creased the jailor with a gun butt and vamoosed," explained the brittle-voiced posseman, apparently the leader. "The coyote grabbed a Frying Pan pony and it's tied by yore water trough."

"Hell!" boomed the tall rider. "One of the boys picked up thet cayuse this forenoon, beyond Lost River, saddle empty and reins adraggin'." There was brief silence, broken by the cowman's voice, "Ef Carson forked thet broomtail, I gamble yuh'll find his carcase out on the flats with a greaser bullet through his conk. Pancho's vaqueros been layin' f'r the jasper."

"Le's give the pony a once-over," suggested a posseman. "Mebbe they's blood on the saddle."

Again boots clumped, as the posse trooped toward the yard. Sound of their voices died. Bill eased the door open a cautious six inches and peered out. Thompson occupied his favorite rocker again, smoking placidly.

"Set in yore hole awhiles," he warned in a low voice. "Them hairpins ain't satisfied, not by a long sight."

Bill stood in the darkness, waiting and listening. Presently, he heard the muted thud of hooves. Fiddlefoot's long form swung into the living room. "Thet bonehaid bunch from town done split the breeze," he announced. "Likewise the Frying Pan pony." His voice became wistful, "Thet shore was a dandy chunk of horseflesh."

Thompson nodded, jerked his head toward the door. Fiddlefoot eased out.

Bill emerged from cover, fumbled with a cigarette to hide his uncertainty. He just couldn't figure the motives of the poker-faced old cowman, smoking calmly in the rocker. Thompson had every reason to see him securely confined behind prison bars again. He had threatened the cowman, had sworn to kill him. A word, a gesture on Thompson's part would have put the possemen wise. But the cowman had shielded him. Why?

"Take the weight off yore laigs," drawled the Boxed T boss. He weighed the young rider with deep-set eyes as Bill stiffly subsided into a chair.

"Yore paw, the gent yuh call Crawler Carson, was Lightnin' Lefevre?" It was plainly a bald statement, rather than a question.

Bill nodded.

"And yuh figger I plugged Lightnin' in the back?"

"Thet's what paw claims."

"Kin Lightnin' still use his guns?"

"Ain't none faster," Bill assured him pridefully.

Thompson thoughtfully sucked his cigarette. " 'Pears thet me and Lightnin' should match cutters, not me 'n you."

"Paw's chained down, way back in Texas. Like I said, his laigs are crippled, bad."

"Wal, mebbe I should go tuh Texas."

Quick hope thrilled the baffled rider. The cowman's calm pronouncement seemed too good to be true. Here was an ideal solution to his problem. Paw craved revenge upon the man who maimed him. What sweeter revenge for the hate-crazed cripple than to toll that man within range of his death-dealing sixes? Then suspicion swirled through him and he said, "Yuh stringin' me?"

"Son," said Thompson slowly, with an intensity of feeling such as he had never displayed before, "ef I could have located Lightnin' Lefevre I'd have braced him long afore yuh made tracks tuh Grass Valley." There was no mistaking the sincerity in the cowman's voice. The young rider remembered the reward notice he had torn from the office wall, "$5,000 Reward, Wanted, Dead or Alive, Lightning Lefevre," signed by James Thompson. Was the cowman playing for the reward money? He quickly discarded the idea. Thompson was rich, plenty rich, owned the best part of Grass Valley. He'd be loco to face Crawler's deadly guns on the chance of collecting a few lousy dollars. No, decided Bill, there was something here that was hidden, something beyond his comprehension. Well, when paw and the cowman got together he might find out—if Thompson lived long enough to talk.

That night he slept in the bunkhouse. For a long while he lay awake, staring at the bullet holes in the ceiling, punched by exuberant waddies seized by an irresistible urge to shoot—when the only safe direction in the crowded bunkhouse was up.

Now that the time had arrived to make a final break with the Valley, he was conscious of a curious reluctance to pull out. Hadn't he every reason, he argued mentally, to be as contented as a kid in a candy store? He was escaping a posse and he was fulfilling his pledge to paw. Grass Valley had brought him nothing but grief. Two near hangings, gunplay aplenty, a couple of spells in jail—it sure had been tough. If they caught up with him, he'd be mighty lucky if he didn't dangle from the nearest tree. Sooner or later, if he stuck around, the law would get him, and that meant a long penitentiary term. He couldn't have tangled his rope worse if he'd tried.

Then Tess Goodmer's face, her pert upturned nose, humorous mouth, challenging gray eyes, floated before him, and he knew full well why he hated to head eastward. Chances were he'd never hit Arizona again. If Thompson, by some mischance, plugged paw, he'd have to kill the cowman—or be ashamed ever to look another man in the eye. When paw cut down the cowman, and nothing seemed surer, he'd settle down to the old life in Panther Gulch. No son worthy of the name could pull out and leave a helpless cripple to battle life alone.

Finally, Bill dropped off into troubled sleep, and dreamed a glorious dream—he had his own iron and a swell spread. There were cows aplenty on the range, carrying his brand; a loyal bunch of rannies in the bunkhouse and Tess rode beside him. His herds increased so rapidly it seemed that all the heifers had twins and the bulls calves. Then, as he sat his pony and eyed his abounding herds from a high bench, a posse emerged from a draw. Yelling, the pursuing riders quirted their ponies and pounded toward him, each man waving a warrant in one hand and throwing lead with the other. Bang—bang—bang—the reports dinned into his ears. He whirled his pony and fled, spurring desperately. But the dread pursuers drew closer, closer. The reports of their six guns were deafening. He found himself in a blind canyon. A mighty wall of rock barred the way. He was cornered. With a groan of hopelessness, he pressed hands against his ears to shut out the incessant clang—clang—clang of gunfire and awoke in a cold sweat. Around him, men were stirring stiffly and swearing, and the clang of Pegleg's cleaver on the angle iron suspended outside the cookhouse door echoed through the spread—Clang! Clang!! Clang!!!

Distant mountains still veiled the rising sun when two riders, tailed by a pack pony, jogged eastward across the swales.

Thompson had lost no time in living up to his word. It was Bill whose feet dragged when the old cowman made preparations for a quick start. As long as he was in the Valley, there was a chance he might see Tess again. A mighty slim chance, cold reason told him. He couldn't venture within gunshot of town, couldn't ride within sight of a stranger. He was a marked man in Grass Valley, and would be a marked man until he died. So he knew well that his reluctance to pull out just didn't make horse sense, and there was no reasonable excuse he could advance that would delay departure. So it was that he rode at the old cowman's stirrup as dismal as a duck in the desert.

The sun silvered Lost River as they crossed the ford. Bill's wistful gaze strayed northeast, where the square squat outline of the butte behind Painted Rock protruded above the horizon. Damn Lady Luck She sure had hashed up his hopes.

Thompson broke a long silence, "A great country, son!"

"Best I ever laid eyes on," agreed Bill fervently.

Pondering over their strange mission, as the plodding ponies ate up the miles, he was amazed to find himself questioning Crawler's judgment. Jim Thompson, according to his crippled paw, was a yellow bushwhacker, a skunk who lacked the guts to fight a man face to face, and struck from behind. Yet instinct and observation told him that the taciturn old cowman by his side was the very opposite type. Thompson could have let him hang, when he was accused of the knifing; he could have betrayed him to the posse the previous night; he could have put a slug in his back when they crossed the river. He had had chances aplenty to get rid of the son of the man he was accused of crippling. But he hadn't done it. Again the perplexed Bill asked, "Why?"

There was only one answer, he mused. Paw must have made a mighty big mistake. Somehow or other, Crawler had sicked him onto the wrong man.

From that moment his antagonism to Jim Thompson began to fade, and it withered quickly. Day after day they worked eastward, climbed lofty mountain passes among the frowning peaks; crawled across arid wastes, where dust devils whirled in ghostly fury; threaded through towering bear grass and thickets of prickly pear, where whitening bones spoke starkly of ever-lurking death. Endlessly, the pair jogged on and on, shrouded by floating dust and scorched by the glaring sun. They sat by lonely campfires, saying little but thinking much; spread their blanket rolls side by side; and a bond grew between them as powerful as it was intangible.

At the last camp before they reached Panther Gulch, Bill voiced a conviction that had grown ever stronger with the passing of the miles, "Thompson, yuh ain't no bushwhacker. Paw done got his ideas twisted. He shore pegged the wrong man."

Across the low-burning buffalo chip fire, the old cowman fixed him with inscrutable blue eyes, "So yore dead shore, son?"

"I'd stake my life on it."

For a while, the older man sat silent, then he spoke, "I got a crazy notion, leastways, it'll sound crazy tuh you. Yuh ride in ahaid. Let on tuh Lightnin' yuh beefed Jim Thompson like he ordered."

The old suspicion awoke in Bill's mind. "Say," he demanded harshly, "what's the shenanigans? Yuh want tuh get paw off guard, so yuh kin plug him—fust?"

"Son," came back the cowman, unruffled, "use yore haid! I coulda beefed yuh a dozen times since we pulled outta Grass Valley, and no one woulda been the wiser. Then I coulda rode on tuh Panther Gulch and laid f'r Lightnin'. Wal, I didn't. Yuh do what I say!"

For a spell, Bill considered this strange request with furrowed brow. Then he nodded, "It don't make sense, but I guess we'll play it yore way."

Growing excitement gripped him when they beat across oak-clothed benches the next morning. Panther Gulch was close now, hidden in the rounded hills ahead. The terrain leveled and the nodding ponies padded through aisles of slim piñon. The trail dipped, and Bill pointed with ill-concealed eagerness to a finger of smoke wavering up through the clear air of the canyon that lay below. "Thet's it!" he ejaculated. "Panther Gulch!"

Thompson pulled rein. Bill handed over the lead rope of the pack pony, pricked his mount to a canter and hit breathlessly down the slope; broke through a screen of brush and emerged into a clearing. "Gosh," he thought, "it ain't changed a mite since I pulled out!"

Crawler, useless legs flopping, huddled in the old armchair, as of yore, set on the shady side of the shack. The scarred piñon stump protruded from the ground like a decayed tooth. Beyond, in the pole corral, Bill glimpsed his sorrel.

With shrill yippee, he shook the Boxed T pony into a gallop, pounded across the familiar flat, reined down in a swirl of dust a dozen paces from the hunched form of Crawler.

"Hi, Paw!" he yelled joyously. "How yuh doin'?"

No pleasure showed in the cripple's pale eyes, glinting from his gaunt features. "And whar yuh been hidin' yoreself?" he snarled.

Bill trailed his reins and strode forward eagerly. "Heck, Paw, thet job took time."

"Yuh plug the bustard?" Crawler's head craned forward upon his shriveled neck, eyes intent, thin lips pursed. Like an evil old buzzard, thought Bill irreverently.

"Shore!"

"He daid?"

"As a can of corned beef."

Bill recoiled before the swift hatred that blazed in the cripple's eyes. The buzzard was now a devil incarnate.

"Most twenty-five years," he croaked. "Twenty-five years, I waited f'r this. Now yuh git yores—yuh son of a bitch!" His crooked fingers, like talons, swept down to the ever-present gun at his side. Like a striking rattlesnake, it arced up and out, a blued blurr in the sunlight. Loose jawed with amazement, Bill stood slackly. Had his paw gone stark, raving mad?

But when Lightning Lefevre threw down there was little time for thought. Helplessly, as though in the throes of a horrible nightmare, Bill saw the hammer drop as the hate-twisted gunman's thumb released it. It was all over in a split second.

CHAPTER TWENTY-ONE

FROM BEHIND, the bewildered Bill heard the drum of hooves and a hoarse shout of warning as Thompson burst out of the brush, spurring madly. At the same instant the hammer dropped and the young rider's nerves quivered as he awaited the smashing impact of a slug.

Nothing happened. The hammer clicked, was cocked again by the frothing Crawler and descended harmlessly for the second time. Then the cripple sighted Jim Thompson hurtling across the clearing. Stark disbelief was mirrored in his distended eyes. A yell, more animal than human, tore from his throat. He hurled his useless gun aside, bony fingers clawing at the air in a paroxysm of inarticulate rage.

Bill gazed numbly at the twisted envenomed features of the man he called paw. Never had he seen such corroding passion mirrored upon a human face. It was the face of a devil—consigned to everlasting torment. Then Crawler screamed!

Thompson brushed past him, stepped close to the writhing, screeching hulk. His close proximity seemed to drive Crawler completely insane. The cripple's wasted legs threshed; foam bubbling from his lips, he half rose from the chair, his clenched fists thrust high. Then, as though the axe of judgment had descended, he collapsed like a pricked balloon across his palsied legs. His head lolled forward and his long arms dangled limp over the sides of the chair.

Bill jumped forward, but the cowman was before him. Thompson raised the wilted form, then let it fall. "A stroke!" he said shortly, and there was no compassion in his eyes.

"Paw musta gone loco," said Bill in subdued tones. He picked up the long-barreled Colt, blew the dust off the cylinder. "It was shore a miracle thet gun misfired," he murmured. "He was dead set tuh kill." Mechanically, he pressed the release key, glanced at the cylinder. "Holy smoke," he ejaculated, "there ain't a bean on the wheel!"

Tiata waddled out of the lean-to kitchen, regarded the dead man with expressionless eyes. "Ugh!" Her deep gutturals expressed satisfaction. "Him bad man—him dead—good!"

"Say, how come his iron was unloaded?" Bill held out the empty cylinder, cradled in his palm.

"Preacher take shell out—Crawler drunk, very drunk. Preacher say bad to kill. Preacher good man—all hell and halleluyah." Tiata's broad, coppery features creased in a rare smile of satisfaction. "He give me ticket to Heaven!"

She dove into the folds of her voluminous dress and produced—a brass bar check!

Thompson chuckled, but Bill's mind was wrestling with the enigma of the empty gun. "What preacher, Tiata? Did he have a black beard and long black hair?"

The squaw nodded, "Um! He ride balky mule."

"Preacher Paul!" muttered Bill. "How in heck did he find his way here?" If it hadn't been for Paul, he'd have taken the long jump, at the hand of a crazy man. Then Bill thought of the gold in the big trunk. With a muttered excuse, he headed for the shack. The interior seemed unchanged and the trunk stood as of old, set against the wall behind Crawler's couch.

Bill threw up the heavy lid, sank onto his knees and delved into the muddle inside—bits of discarded saddlery, shirts, cartridge belts, old guns, boots. But he groped in vain for the feel of the hard leather pouches, stuffed with double eagles, that had been stacked beneath the litter.

"What in thunder," he thought confusedly, "was the preacher's play?" He straightened, and as his head came up, he glimpsed a sheet of paper, tacked inside the upraised trunk top. It was covered with writing, in a bold, sprawled hand. Wondering, he read:

> Friend Bill:
>
> Seek and ye shall find, so sayeth the Good Book. I have sought and I have found. In return for your cooperation I may have saved your life. In days long past, when I was young and trusting, even as you, Lightning was my idol. He 'crossed me, as he 'crossed everyone—even as he 'crossed you.
>
> Adios!
> Paul.

Still foundering mentally, Bill noticed the impression of type from the reverse side of the sheet. He turned it over, and gazed at an ancient Wanted notice, carrying the picture of a hawk-nosed young man with piercing eyes. It was Paul the Preacher, short-haired and beardless. With absorbed interest, Bill scanned the printed words:

> WANTED
> $1,000 Reward
>
> Samuel Larson, alias Scripture Sam. Height 6' 2"; weight 180 lbs. Age 22. Black hair, hook nose. Member of notorious Lefevre gang. Fast with gun. Well educated, trained for the Ministry.
>
> James Thompson,
> Sheriff, Laramine County,
> Texas

So the preacher was a crook! What next?

Bill dropped the trunk lid, stepped outside. Thompson stood silently surveying the crumpled form of Lightning Lefevre.

"Lamp this!" invited the young rider, extending Paul's scrawled message. The cowman glanced over it, reversed the sheet and read the Wanted notice. His broad shoulders shook with inward laughter. "So Scripture Sam's back on his old stamping ground! When we busted up the gang he lit out f'r South America. Thet jasper's slicker'n a greased hawg."

"What I don't get," said Bill, frowning, "is thet crack about paw 'crossin' me." He eyed the gunman's remains somberly. Crawler might have been as dangerous as a mad dog, but he was his father.

"Paw! Whar d'yuh git thet idea?" drawled Thompson.

Bill's head came up with a jerk. He eyed the cowman sharply. "Hell," he blurted, "don't tell me you gone loco, too!"

"Never was more levelhaided in my life, son. Le's squat awhiles in the shade, while I loosen my yawp." Thompson led the way to the wall of the shack, hunkered against it. Bill sank down beside him.

For a full minute, the old cowman stared at the blue outlines of distant mountains, then he began to build a smoke and to talk: "Around twenty-five years back, son, I was sheriff of Laramine County. Texas was shore wild and woolly in them days. Lightnin' Lefevre was uncrowned king of the border gangs. He was lightnin' on the draw, as cold-blooded as a bullfrog and as crooked as a dawg's hind laig. He raised hell along the Border—histin' banks, holdin' up stages, raidin' ranches, any devilment thet paid a dollar.

"I hunted Lightnin' like a lobo, came nigh tuh cornerin' the bustard, but he always slipped away. He crippled Fiddlefoot's fist in one fracas—best deputy I ever had. Wal, I run him outta the country and busted up the gang, beefed most of 'em. I clean fergot Lefevre, had plenty more trouble on my hands. But Lefevre never fergot me. Thet rattlesnake could hold a grudge longer than any man I know—and how he hated my guts!

"Wal, one night I was called out tuh go downtown and stop a saloon fracas. As soon as I left the house a masked hombre busted in and slugged yore maw. She had plenty sand. Her haid was busted in, but she grabbed my shotgun. Emptied it at the lobo, but he knocked the barrel aside.

"I heard the report and hotfooted back, jest in time tuh lamp the jasper spurrin' off. He was packin' a bundle—I never dreamed it was you—and threw a slug after him. Thet's how Crawler, as you call him, was crippled f'r life.

"Wal, I busted inter the house and yore maw's stretched out on the kitchen floor. She died within the hour, but she tore the mask off'n the rattlesnake and whispered thet Lefevre had grabbed you. I was most loco with grief—hotfooted f'r the sawbones. Then I looked in yore crib tuh make shore—it was empty!"

"I hunted Lefevre f'r months, quit sheriffin' so as I'd hev more time. Me and Fiddlefoot combed the Border, but it seemed like Lefevre and my kid had jest melted inter thin air.

"I couldn't abide Texas after thet. I rode west, into Apache country and located near Painted Rock, which was jest a stockaded tradin' post. Time passed. I built up the spread and adopted thet gal, thought mebbe she'd fill the gap thet you and yore maw left. But she never fergot her folks—and never forgive me f'r wipin' 'em out. She musta hated me plenty, f'r she knifed me the night you hit the Boxed T.

"Fiddlefoot put me wise afore you rode in. I told him he was loco. It jest didn't seem possible thet the baby Lefevre snatched most twenty-five years afore could be alive. But the moment I set eyes on you, son, I knew! Yuh got thet birthmark under yore left eye, yuh got blue eyes, stocky frame—hell, yore a Thompson from tip tuh toe." He glanced at the sober-faced Bill, who was intently absorbing every word. "I'm runnin' off plenty at the mouth. Want I should quit?"

"Go right ahaid—paw!" The young rider's voice was husky.

"When yuh called me out, I most died. Right then, I figgered it was more of Lefevre's deviltry. So I played f'r time. Ain't many tangles thet won't straighten out, son, ef yuh give 'em a chance. Me, I reckon I learned patience the hard way."

Bill spat out the sodden remnants of his cigarette, started to make another. "Yuh crippled Lefevre, unbeknown, with thet shot in the dark," he ruminated, half to himself, "and he was chained down, f'r life. So he went tuh earth and raised me—to kill you. Then, when he figgered I'd beef yuh, he let me have it—tuh wipe out the Thompson clan complete. Gosh! The lousy, double-crossin', yeller-gutted buzzard! Wal, I shore gotta thank the preacher f'r hornin' in."

The older man nodded. "Yep, I tangled my spurs. I never looked f'r Lightnin' tuh plug you. I jest thought he'd come clean—mock yuh f'r killin' yore own paw. But he was shore pison—tuh the last."

Tiata had no wish to leave Panther Gulch. They left her with a saddle pony and ample supplies, content with the knowledge that there would be a remittance at the bank in San Andreas every month as long as she lived to draw it.

Father and son sat by the first campfire on the long ride back to Grass Valley. The old cowman brushed aside Bill's misgivings anent the warrant charging bank robbery and horse theft that probably awaited him at Painted Rock. "Don't amount to a damn, son," he drawled. "Jack Goodmer's on the mend, he kin swear yuh had no part in the bank histin'. And as f'r thet cayuse, I done owned the Frying Pan, lock, stock and barrel, these six months. The Limey's got itchy feet, craves tuh make tracks f'r California. So, in a way of speakin', yuh done stole yore own hawse."

Bill gazed into the leaping flames, saw a coppery-haired girl with tantalizing gray eyes. "Thet Frying Pan spread, it ain't a bad little outfit, Paw," he began tentatively.

"Heck, son, ef it warn't good, I wouldn't hev bought it!"

"Dandy house, good water, plenty range," mused Bill, seized by an absorbing idea.

Thompson eyed his new-found son humorously, "Yuh ain't thinkin' of batchin'?"

"Heck no!" ejaculated Bill, engrossed by the entrancing vision that was growing in his mind. He roused as he became aware that his father was eyeing him intently.

"D'yuh figger," he inquired, with elaborate casualness, "we could ride back by way of Painted Rock. I'm kinda bothered about Jack Goodmer, guess he's mighty puny."

"Thet's shore thoughtful of yuh, son." Thompson's voice was grave, but there was a twinkle in his deep-set eyes. "At yore age I'd be a mite more bothered about thet redhaided sister of his."

"Quit funnin', Paw!"

Their eyes met.

As one, they grinned—with complete understanding.

www.ingramcontent.com/pod-product-compliance
Lightning Source LLC
LaVergne TN
LVHW050958080826
845145LV00009B/2338